10 SHORT STORIES FOR YOUNG ADULTS

AMARVANI

Acknowledgements

I would like to express my gratitude to my family for bearing me so far. It's a rare quality of metaphysical torture that only they can describe since I live with them!

I would like to thank my friends who always believed in me. It means a lot- having someone around who believes in you, in your future, in your potential. They listened to my long lectures on many subjects and made me feel that I make sense!

I would like to thank the people who made a fool of me during my growing up years since I would have never learnt what I learnt had it not been because of them. I would like to thank every person who rejected me for it only strengthened my resolve to make something of my life.

I would like to thank the man in the mirror. He has been there for me, telling me that no matter how much they criticize me, one day, I will realise my dreams. This book is the beginning.

Thanks to everyone I met on the way.

This book is a product of author's imagination and life's experiences. The readers have the right to disagree and form their own opinions. Even this book, like any other, is a point of view.

-Amar

Introduction

Dear Readers,

The book that you have in your hand marks the beginning of my writing career. There is a lot I have to share with you. It is a compilation of some of the most powerful thoughts that have crossed my mind over the last few years as I started making sense of life.

I have presented my beliefs using stories and/or poems with every chapter.

I will tell you why you should read this book. You should read it for it will get you thinking. That's the best thing I do- getting people to think. That will be the purpose of my writing.

Read it. Somewhere in the book, you will find connections to your life story.

Thank you for your time and effort. I value you and cannot convey in words how important you are to me.

I hope you enjoy the book as much as I enjoyed writing it.

My Regards,

Amar

Table of Contents

1. Today   7

2. Hope   14

3. Friendship   20

4. Love   26

5. Women   46

6. Education and Work   57

7. Competition   71

8. Adversity   84

9 Retire   94

10. Death   102

1. Today

"Live for today-there will never be another one like it."
- The Monk who sold his Ferrari

"Someone should tell us, right at the start of our lives that we are dying. Then we might live life to the limit, every minute of every day. Do it! I say. Whatever you want to do, do it now! There are only so many tomorrows."
-Michael Landon

Today, this day is the most important possession we have. By the time tomorrow comes, this day would be passed and you will never have it again. Enjoy it. Make the most of it. At least live with this realisation.

I have a personal reason for starting this book with this chapter. For majority of my life hitherto, I have been one of those people who did not learn to live for today. I have been someone who lived for a day that will make me happy. And I am telling you this since I know many people who belong of this category.

Why did it happen?

I was taught that you must sacrifice your present for your future. That I must keep working for a distant future and when I achieve it, I have the right to be happy. Before that, I cannot be happy. Sacrifice the present. Sacrifice one day after another and one year after another.

I ended in the company of people who said, "We will live life one day, when we finish college, when we find a job, when this happens, when that happens and life kept slipping by..."

I am so surprised that it did not dawn on me how foolish I was. It took a lot many years and tremendous amount of pain for me to realise that how wrong I have been.

Today is the only day you can really live. Yesterday is gone. Tomorrow is not guaranteed.

I think I was 24 years when I was reading the last chapter of the legendary book, "The Monk Who sold his Ferrari" by Robin Sharma. I remember crying like someone who has just realised losing someone extremely serious- time.

Even after reading it, it took another couple of years for the lessons to sink in. It was hard, very hard. Life teaches everyone differently. I have had to pay for all my lessons.

I like to say that there are very few absolute truths on earth. Most statements can be challenged. May be science will make further advances in future and this may also change. But, as things stand now, no one can refute this truth that we may die anytime.

We need to accept that death could be very close. You may live for 100 years. You may die tomorrow.

When I was in my final year of undergraduate studies, I sold life insurance for a brief period of time to make some money. They are right who they say that selling life insurance is one of the toughest things to do.

Why?

It is because people do not accept that they are going to die anytime. They argue with the entire rationale of life insurance. This happens because they are living in denial.

The greatest pain I have experienced in my growing up years is that somehow most people I met hold the belief that we should postpone life, postpone enjoying life, to another day. We are taught to select a goal and sacrifice your present- a month, a year, 10 years to attain that goal while making your life miserable during the process of the attainment of that goal.

What use is a life we do not spend to live? What use is a life lived in expectation that we will live it someday?

Live like you will die tonight.

Roshan was a bright kid. He was a consistent topper in primary school and loved to play table tennis, cricket and chess.

His parents were both employed and found difficulty in finding time to spend with him. Like most Indian parents, they wanted to see him succeed and outdo the other kids of the locality, the city, and whatever else they could think of.

Roshan was always under pressure from his parents to stay at the top. He could not even ever come at the second place. He knew that he will have to face severe rebuke from his parents in case he ever dropped from the top and he dreaded that. He had a sister also but the pressure on her was milder.

She was a girl and not much was to be expected of her.

His parents did not think that he should waste time on games and activities. They had been extremely hard working and did not have a life beyond books during their school years. As a result, Roshan hardly got time for games and activities.

Roshan's parents were Chartered Accountants. "It is extremely difficult to become a chartered accountant in India," he had heard.

He remembered his father telling him once, "You have no idea Roshan, how hard I had to work to become a chartered account and so did your mother. The success rate is only 1%. That means out of every 100 people who apply to become a chartered accountant, only 1 succeeds. You see. Do you understand? I cleared all the exams in one single shot and your mother had to appear for her final exams thrice, but she also made it. I helped her to crack the final exams. Actually, that's when she fell for me. But that's not the point. The point is that we had to work extremely hard to become what we are. That should inspire you to work hard also. I want you to become a chartered accountant also. Otherwise, what will people say? See, that son of chartered accountants, he could not make anything of his life. See, he came second! What will society think of us?!"

Roshan's parents provided him with every material support they could. He had a chauffeur to drop him to school, to tuitions and bring back home. He had all the material comforts, but slowly Roshan's performance started to fall.

He topped his school till standard 8th but he came second in class 9th final exams and all hell broke loose!

"How could do you this?! What happened? Why did you not tell us earlier that something like that is likely? We would have provided you with all the resources you needed. Roshan, where did we fall short?" his father shouted, incredulously.

Roshan looked at his father and he did not know what to say. He was sobbing. His mother was undecided how to react to the situation. She thought that she agreed with her husband.

Roshan entered standard class 10th with higher pressure on him. His father had asked his mother to make sure that Roshan must never fall from the top spot again.

Unfortunately for the family, his performance kept deteriorating and in the term examinations, Roshan was 3rd from last! He did not know how to face his parents after the results were announced.

He reached home that day and slept in his room without telling anything to anybody. However, he realised that he could not hide the news for long since his parents had been invited to the parents and teachers meeting scheduled on the following weekend.

He was shivering when he went to see the results with his father. He knew what the result was. What he could not face was the reaction of his father. He did not know how he would bear what will follow once his father knows of the results. He fell unconscious at the gate of the school.

Everyone gathered on the spot and they felt that Roshan must have had a heat stroke. He was taken to the hospital when he could not be resuscitated on the spot.

Roshan did not wake up, ever again. He was declared brought dead. No one could understand it. Roshan was dead. His body was sent for autopsy and no concrete results could be arrived at by the doctors.

His parents were shocked completely unable to figure out, what happened to Roshan.

One person had known. Roshan's little sister. She knew that Roshan was killed systematically, he had been denied a childhood by the strain on the little shoulders, pain of expectations he could not bear, anymore."

He was not allowed to live a single day of his life since he began schooling. He was always told to keep working to stay at the top. He was taught to sacrifice his present. He could not take it."

End of story

Roshan would not have died if his parents allowed him to live his childhood. If they told him to take it easy and explore life the way he likes and be around to guide him. His life was wasted one day after another and one day, he just could not take it anymore.

I could not find the name of the great man who wrote the following words, but they mean a lot to my mind. Read them once. Read them again and apply the lesson if it appeals to your sense of logic.

The Moment

"I May never see tomorrow there's no written guarantee, and things that happened yesterday belong to history. I cannot predict the future, I cannot change the past. I have just the present moment; I must treat it as my last. I must use this moment wisely, for it soon will pass away, and be lost to me forever as part as yesterday.

I must exercise compassion, help the fallen to their feet, be a friend unto the friendless, make an empty life complete. The unkind things I do today may never be undone, and the friendships that I fail to win, may nevermore be won. I may not have another chance, on bended knees to pray and thank God with humble heart, for giving me this day."

-anonymous

THE DAY VISION

I am up before the dawn breaks
I run as the dark fades

I sleep a little allowing my body and senses to unwind
I eat a little nourishing my soul, body and mind

Laziness knocked, I left it unheard
Energy is my name, Vibrant is my word

I love my past, everything has had a reason
The lessons have made me what I have become
Spring is my favourite and I love every season

Future will be as I see it or better still
I am sure I am yet to see my best
I believe I can I think I will

I stick to the truth
Sweet or bitter; harsh or pretty
I do as I say, my word is my integrity

I work for over half a day
Do what I believe is not work but play
What I do defines me not money, people, and name
The best is the standard and play I do to win the game

I smile every second just for the sake of cheer and grace
No one changed a thing on earth with a frown, tense and grumpy face

I love life and I love living

This day on earth is such a gift

If there is god I pray

Grant me what it takes to make most of it!

-   Amar

2. Hope

I believe that hope is the most beautiful word in English Language.

Hope. There is something that happens when I say that word, softly. Try it. Say it, hope.

Hope is enmeshed in life, as it is. As I write this, I am reminded of the catastrophe in Haiti where thousands of people have died in one of the worst natural disasters mankind has seen. There is still hope that nature has had its expression of anger and Haitians will be able to resume life to normal. The ones, who will survive, will rebuild a new life- build it on hope.

For us, human beings, as long as we are alive, anything can come to an end- the jobs we stick to so dearly for they pay for our lives, our relationships, businesses. Almost everything that's dear to us can come to an end.

Thankfully, we can start again. As long as we are breathing, it's not over.

Hopefully, things would be better again and life will be happier.

Do not ever give up hope. It's all we have.

Let me tell you a story.

"Sujoy had turned 27 just a week back.

He was sitting quietly facing the river with his legs immersed in water-thinking about his life. He was happy for he had achieved success much beyond what was expected of him. It did not always seem possible or easy. He was himself not sure, many times. But he had always been hopeful.

He was now an engineer and had a salary of Rs. 80000 a month, an extremely respectable salary in India. He had a beautiful wife whom he loved a lot and his parents were proud of him. As he sat amused with himself, he looked back.

Sujoy belonged to a small town in India.

His parents were poor and had worked extremely hard to make sure that he received good education and does not have to go through the physical drudgery that had been their lives.

Sujoy's parents ironed clothes to make a living ever since he remembered. They would go to collect clothing items from the houses in the precinct where they worked, in the morning, iron them all day and then deliver the ironed clothes in the evening. That was how their lives were spent, almost the entire lives.

He saw them working day and night in the *hope* that one day, when he becomes something, they will be proud and their efforts would have paid off. They did not know what exactly he will become. Their definition of success for him was a job that paid him at least Rs 15000 a month.

When Sujoy thought about his parents, he realised that they had never asked or wished for anything for them and had devoted entire lives to his upbringing. He remembered asking his father once, "Papa, why don't you go and buy some handsome clothes for yourself?"

"I do not need any, I am happy to see you in the best of clothing and that is enough for me," his father said.

"Are all parents like this?" he had thought. His mother would mostly subscribe to the opinions of his father. He did not remember her ever asserting views of her own.

He did not have any siblings. He had wondered, "Why?" and had assumed the answer that his parents had been wise enough. It was better only to have children you can support rather to send them begging!

His childhood had been tough. Sometimes, with the studies, he would help his parents with ironing or delivering the ironed clothes to the customers. His friends at school were helpful and considerate towards him.

There had been certain very difficult moments when Sujoy did not have the will to move forward and he felt like he would give up.

One of such incidents was that of his mother falling prey to anaemia. Sujoy was 15 then. His mother was in the bed for months and was not recuperating for a long time. His father had to attend to work and there were many days he was not able to go to school and stayed with his ailing mother in the hospital. The medical expenses had been exorbitant to be borne by their family and this had resulted in an acute sense of helplessness.

His father kept very quiet during the entire episode and Sujoy knew how difficult it was for his father. He was a strongly built man but Sujoy felt that that he looked pale during the period his mother was sick.

"What if something happens to maa?" the thought had chilled every bone in Sujoy's body as he sat besides his mother. He did not think of school for many days as he stayed absent because somebody was needed at his mothers' bedside and they had no relatives to support them. All he did was pray and hoped that everything would be fine.

His mothers' health improved after staying in the hospital for about a month and going through multiple transfusions of blood. They had survived, survived on hope.

He had finished school in the next 2 years and secured admission to an engineering college in his state itself. But he had to leave home to a different city. It had been killing to stop his mother from crying when he left home. His father had been calm as usual. They knew that this was the last straw. He will finish his engineering and come back home.

The duration of his course was 4 years. He was doing well and working very hard. His home city was at a distance of 5 hours distance from his engineering school.

He lived there with one other boy called Shakti who shared the room with him. Initially they had not liked each other but after a couple of arguments and altercations, they had become very close friends. Sujoy was very happy to have Shakti as a friend. He felt grateful for his presence.

In the 2nd year, he had an accident and he fractured his left ankle. His 4th semester exams had been due and he did not know what to do and how would he finish the courses and prepare for the exams. He was feeling broken and when he saw his plastered leg, he cried and cried some more. The expenses were covered under the insurance which was a part of the fees.

He did not tell his parents about the incident initially. Shakti insisted that he should inform his parents but he did not budge. But he did not succeed for long in hiding it from his mother who could sense that something was wrong. She asked him, "Sujoy, what's wrong with you? You do not sound yourself." And he broke down.

Sujoy realised that he will not be able to hide anything from his mother. He told her and his parents came over to see him. His mother wept when she looked at him but he asked her to stay calm when he himself was in agony.

Shakti spoke to the headmaster to allow Sujoy to miss the classes and take the examination. The headmaster did not approve and this caused him extreme anguish. He had thought, "What's the point of it all?"

His father went again to the headmaster to make a special exemption in his case on the basis of his sincere record so far. The college governing council considered the issue and finally he was allowed to take the exams and not miss a semester.

He recovered in 3 months and things returned to normal.

There had been many such incidents, Sujoy thought, where he felt that life will not recover from the shock like getting fired from his first job within 2 months, the break up from his first relationship which emotionally devastated him but he had recovered and those incidents had proved to be transitory. He had emerged being hopeful and successful. He had gifted a car to his parents last year. Life was just beginning as he got married a month back.

His wife returned with food and both of them sat eating and splashing water with their feet, looking at the horizon."

End of story

Sometimes things will not work. These are the times we need to hold on, as human beings. We must hold on. Tough times don't last.

Hope does.

Things will happen. Life is a concoction of problems. You can call them challenges if that makes you feel better. There will be times in your life when you will feel devastated as if everything is over.

You will meet new people, you will meet better people, and you will have chances to turn your life around only if you keep hope.

Hope. It is the most beautiful word in English language.

Hope. For you want to fight and you are not a loser.

Hope. For history has proved over and over again that people who do not give up hope and keep on working towards their goals eventually succeed.

Hope. For those who love you and still need you.

Hope. For tomorrow is another day.

Hope. For it's a beautiful life.

Hope

At times I think, when things are not good,
At times I think, when gloom clouds my mood,
At times I think, in overwhelming pain,
At times I think when all seems in vain.

I think at times – is it worth it!
I think at times – does it all matter!

True these emotions are;
No lie that life is in shatters,
But I am living and,
and that is actually what matters.

There are people who love me;
there are those who need me.
There are mountains to climb;
there are things to be done.
There are reasons to believe that,
Life still is fun.

Yes, I am hurt, I am torn apart,
but nothing stops me from making a new start.
So let's perform duties, walk that tight rope,
because I am living and there is Hope.

3. Friendship

I have grown up thinking about what the term 'friend' means to me. Most of us of like to think that we have a lot of friends, don't we?

When I was a young child, I thought everyone I spoke to and who spoke to me was my friend. Ha! I laugh at myself when I think about it. Not that I am any richer in terms of number of friends now, at 28. Surprisingly, the number of people I call 'friends' has only reduced with time.

Here is my definition of a friend-

A friend is a person I want to be a friend to

Now, this is it. This definition puts the responsibility on me and that's what I like. I like responsibility. I decide if I would like to be someone's friend.

And once I do, I do whatever it takes to maintain that relationship for I love my friends. I value my friends a lot since they are most special people outside my family. They make my life worth living. They make it worth fighting for. They mean a lot to me.

I am grateful at this point in time to have some really wonderful friends. I respect each and every one of them for the kind of people that they are. My friends are the best people I know. I am proud of being able to call them so.

I am emphasizing this point because I think it is very important to our sense of world view and life who we decide are our friends. Outside our immediate families, they are the most important people on earth.

In order to lead a beautiful life, we do not need people who have all the right credentials. We need people who 'care.' Wow! What a beautiful word is it! Isn't it? We want to care. We want people who care.

In the pandemonium of life, we need people who understand us, who may not agree with us, but they listen, empathise and give us a feeling that world is a nice place to live in.

Friends make the world a lovelier, a loving and an understanding place.

Life would have been so lonely otherwise.

The greatest disease plaguing human kind is not AIDS or Swine Flu or Malaria. It is loneliness. It is spreading in our society like wild fire. People do not talk to each other anymore. The richer people get, they seem to prefer more isolation. There is a major trust deficit in the society.

Nevertheless, take the risk. Take the risk of talking to someone new. Someone you think you will like. Someone to whose life you can contribute. Someone you enjoy talking to. Someone who values your time and the attention you give him.

Go make a friend. Be a friend.

"Victor belonged to a filthy rich family. Filthy! He had wondered why people call it that way. Why is it filthy to be rich?! The answer had eluded him.

His father was a businessman, a builder. His ancestors owned many acres of land in India and his father had inherited it. He knew that he would be the next claimant to the wealth.

There generally would be many visitors to the house and he would see people coming to visit and please his father. They lived in a posh locality of New Delhi. His mother was a housewife. Since his father was a busy man, he did not spend quality time with him. He had seen his father work very hard, almost 7 days of the week and he would occasionally enquire from him how his studies were going, although the discussion seemed perfunctory to Victor. He had grown weary about it over the years and stopped paying much attention to it.

He did not regard his mother to be a lady of high intellect. Since she was his mother, he loved and respected her as she did to him, but unfortunately for him, he could not talk much with her, since he felt that she would not be able to understand him. She would spend a lot of her time with her friends whom she would meet at kitty parties in the city and she would have such parties pretty often.

Victor was now 17 years old and studied in an eminent school in the city meant for the filthy rich. He was not a very talkative boy in school. Although he was a good student, but since he knew that one day, he will be joining his father in business, he did not pay much attention to studies. He was satisfied with the scores that he received and did not make a fuss about it. His parents also felt that he should be doing fine and did not bother!

He was in standard 11th and since he had to choose either science/commerce/arts after as was the norm in his school, he had chosen commerce. The general perception about commerce was that it was easier than science. So, that prompted him to choose it. He did not want to study arts. He did not think that he had any artistic streak in him.

Victor was shy boy. He would not talk to any of his classmates until prompted. Not many people noticed him. He used to feel what they might think of him. He wanted to talk to someone who would understand him, his life, what he would like to do, but he could not conjure up the courage to talk. He had no friends.

So his life had been a monotonous routine- going to school every morning, spending 7-8 hours there attending classes, coming home to rest for a while and spend the evening attending tuitions.

Wherever he went, he felt like talking more with his peers but he could not find the courage to do it.

He used to like swimming in a club where his father was a member and that entitled membership to the entire family. He would go there in the evening sometimes, whenever he would get time away from his tuitions. One day, on his visit, he met Raman, the new student in his class, who had just joined this school since Raman's father had shifted to New Delhi from Bombay.

Raman started talking to Victor. Victor was slow in his responses but he responded to all his questions and also managed to ask him a few questions. That day, when Victor came back home, he thought that he had found a friend.

Next day in school, when Victor saw Raman in the class, he said, "Hi Raman, how are you. It was great meeting you yesterday. May be we should meet often."

"Sure, why not?" Raman responded.

Raman was the most outspoken and extrovert person Victor had met. Within two months of his arrival in school, he started participating in events and activities and making his presence felt. Victor was also learning new things from Raman. They would meet at the pool often and spend time talking about their lives.

One day, Raman asked Victor, "You do not talk much Victor, do you? I have not seen you taking part in competitions and events. Do you not feel like doing it? It's fun. It makes you confident and is a very important part of our learning. I would like to help you if you like."

Victor said, "I would like to, Raman, but I have not been able to do so ever. I have not had the confidence to do it. This is the first time I am telling this to anyone. You are my friend Raman and I am so happy that I have met you. With your help, I think I will be able to change."

Slowly, Victor started to change. He participated in a speech competition. He did not win but the feeling amazed him. He started talking with the rest of his classmates and starting conversations. Everyone started liking him even more.

He scored 70% marks in standard 11th and he was happy with it. Again, his parents did not bother.

Raman congratulated him and said, "Great job buddy, I am sure you can do even better than this. I think this was a great year for you as you made a mark for yourself in many competitions also." Victor felt like a victor.

He was a popular boy in his school now and had other friends also but Raman was closest and he knew how much Raman meant to him.

When Raman fell sick 3 months into the second term, Victor could not bear it. Victor would go to meet Raman at his home and make sure that he does not feel lonely. Raman suffered from recurrent fever for almost a month and that period strengthened their bond of friendship.

Raman recovered and said to Victor, "thank you my friend, you meant a lot to me during this tough period."

"You have no idea Raman, what you mean to me. I may not have understood life if I did not meet you. Thanks."

They graduated from school together and got admission in the same college in the University of Delhi.

Life has been wonderful for Victor. His friends like him and complain that he talks a lot! He fell in love. His parents have no clue what happened to him. They wonder if he has been on drugs. Victor thinks that they like the change since they could not care to ask him."

End of story

How do you go about making friends? Learn from Raman. Dale Carnegie, the author of *how to make friends and influence people* said,

"If you want to make a friend, be a friend. It takes time, energy, faithfulness and selflessness."

<u>Friends</u>

They understand me, they listen to my chatter

When I talk to them, if feels that no problem really matters

They will find the time for me

I know they will, they will not be busy

They make me believe that I will succeed one day

They think I am good and one day I will find the way

I like them a lot, I know they are aware

My friends are precious to me

For I know that they care

4. Love

Love is the most illogical and irrational thing to happen to human beings.

There is hardly anything explicable about it. It is experiential. It is spiritual.

To talk about love, I will divide it into 4 sections:

4.1 Loving your parents

Do you understand your parents? I don't.

I think that I am one of the craziest children anyone could have. But there is one thing I know and I know it very, very well. My parents will stand by me whenever something untoward happens. They always have and I know they will, even now. I think that love is a verb and I know that my parents love me.

I have faced some extremely difficult times during my growing up years, although I am far from being a grown up man even now. I refuse to grow up. It's optional, anyways.

Whenever things got tough, they stood by me and I felt guilty inside, feeling that they should not. There were times that I felt that I did not deserve their love and why should they bother? But they did.

May be, I do not understand this right now because I am not a father. But, it's insane love. I consider myself a messenger of logic. I respect reason and fail to understand the lack of it. I have given up my efforts to find anything rational about love.

I bow to the love of my parents and I love them.

I completely, absolutely despise people who have no respect for their parents and I condemn them in totality. I have known people in my environment who have given no respect for their parents in their twilight years and treated with them in shocking ways. I think these people deserve nothing.

I understand that we will have thought-level differences with our parents. We will, definitely. Since the world has evolved drastically in the last 15 years and people like me who have grown up in these times tend to think differently.

But that by no ways means that you throw your parents out of their own homes and let them die alone somewhere in oblivion!

"Prasad was born in Delhi, India. He was the only child of his parents and was born after 5 years of his parents' married life. They had prayed at many temples for a child and had felt their prayers had been answered when Prasad was born.

His father used to work as a clerk with the Indian government and did not make a lot of money. He has been an honest and sincere man. His mother supported the family financially by giving tuitions to primary school children.

His parents worked very hard to make ends meet in an expensive city like Delhi and made sure that made sure that their son got the best of education and became a successful man. That had been their only ambition from their dull and monotonous life.

Prasad was good at studies and was an avid cricketer also. He won many tournaments for his school. His parents always supported him and never made him get a sense of the financial troubles they went through. They had a tough time arranging for the school fees and training fees for the Cricket Academy, but somehow they managed to make it.

They were very proud of their son and happy that he had been progressing well in life. They would sing laurels about Prasad's achievements to everyone they know. Their jobs had only been the means to an end and find money to educate their only child. It did not mean anything more.

Prasad grew up to be a manager with a Multi- national firm. He had just finished his MBA and he was hired from the campus.

His parents were elated. His mother would go around telling everyone how happy she was for her son and his father allowed himself a tad of arrogance. They felt that their efforts had paid off and all the pain had been redeemed.

Prasad's father organised a party and invited their family and friends to celebrate the success of their son.

"Today, I feel at the top of the world, Prasad. I am so happy that you have done us proud. Although I was confident about you, but there were some times when I had insecurities about your future. All the doubts have melted away today and you have not let us down. I am sure your mother is also elated beyond measure today, although she will not say much. Well done, my boy", Prasad's father said to him at the end of the party.

"Thank you, Papa; I am also very happy that things have worked so positively." He said nothing else that would please his parents on this important occasion.

Prasad had fallen in love with a girl during his MBA and now he wanted to marry her. He shared this thought with his father. The girl was not from the same caste, which is generally, a very important matter in Indian households. His parents although apprehensive of the idea, relented since the issue at stake was Prasad's happiness and they would not be dogmatic.

The girls' family was very pleased with Prasad and his success and had no problems with the marriage.

The marriage was decided and Prasad got married within months. The girls' family was fairly rich and gave a handsome dowry, although Prasad's family did not ask for any.

"We are giving everything for our daughter itself and after all, Prasad is our son also", the girl's mother had insisted.

Prasad's wife- Rachna was an attractive girl or at least Prasad thought so. She had married Prasad because she fell in love with him and they spent a lot of time during the MBA to study each other as well.

However, since she came from a richer family, she found it difficult to adjust to Prasad's house. She was also working and decided that she would not spend any of her time doing housework of any sort.

Prasad's father had retired by now and spent a lot of time reading and sleeping. His mother had stopped giving tuitions five years back and she now spent most of her time in attending to the house. They felt that they have worked enough for the whole of their lives and now it was time to rest.

They had no idea that life was going to become even more difficult for them. Prasad started spending most of his time in office and would come home irritated to sleep. Rachna had similar behaviour with rudeness added to it.

They started feeling extremely angry about it and faced it for a few months as it became almost expected. Then, one day, Prasad's father decided to confront him and try to understand what was happening.

"Prasad, this was not what we have expected! You have no time for us at all and Rachna is even rude to us! What are we to do and what have we done to deserve this?"

"Papa, it's none of Rachna's fault. Please do not say anything to her. She comes back home so tired everyday and then has to listen to you and mummy and what is she expected to do?

They had a long argument which caused immense pain to Prasad's father. They stopped complaining but the status quo remained.

Suddenly, one day, Prasad came to tell his father that he and his wife have had enough of the chaos and had decided to move out.

Prasad's mother started crying and could not stop herself. She was a shy lady and did not have the courage to say anything to her grown up son anymore. Perhaps she just did not expect anything of him, anymore.

They knew that Rachna was the reason for what was happening and she had triggered this decision. But they were not angry with Rachna; they were angry and disappointed with their son for not being able to stand by them.

They left.

Prasad's parents lived alone and Prasad had not visited them even once after leaving.

End of story

There are many similarities to this story to the world we live in.

We are what we are because of the sacrifices and love of our parents. They may have been sceptical at times and their ways may be different, but I can say this with one percent certainty that our parents could have never thought ill of us in their wildest dreams.

Love your parents and be grateful for their love and their presence. Do not take them for granted. When you were growing up, they made sure that you were cared for.

When they grow down, they will need us the most.

Mother's day

Maa was perhaps the first word I learnt to say
She has seen me since as I grew, never shirking her duties in any way
The most inexplicable relation in the world
The deepest at every stage, at every layer
Nothing I could do that could diminish her love
That could take away her care

I am not sure how good a son I have been
She has been selfless, loving and keen
She would sit in front of me just looking at me as I finish my food
She would do all to make sure I can say to the world that I am doing good

The relation between a mother and a child will always be sacred
A mother loves would love and protect her child
Even if he is the greatest idiot!

There are so many relations in this world
So brittle, so fragile
But one relation which you can always be certain of
Is that of a mother and a child?

One person I am sure would be always happy to see me
One person I am sure who would always love me
One person I am sure would always wait for me
One person I am sure would tell the world of my achievements
One person I want to make really proud and happy
Is my mother
I hope it's the same for you!!!

-amar

4.2 Loving your Partner

Love will not always last. Be thankful that it happened. I feel sorry for people who have never been courageous enough to feel the feel of love. Take a risk. There is nothing more beautiful to life.

-   *Amar*

Falling in love is the gooiest, tickling and ethereal feelings one can experience.

There have been a few days in my life that I have never been able to forget. One such day was when I said 'I love you' for the first time in my life. I could not bear the exhilaration of that feeling of having been able to express that it. I loved it then. I love it now whenever the thought of it comes to my mind. I meant it. I became a different person since that day.

It is extremely difficult to explain the rush in your veins and cells when you fall in love with someone who falls in love with you. You have got to feel it. You have got to face it. Or miss living the best life has to offer.

The problem with love is that it may not last forever- even till the end of your life. We have got to be mature enough to be able to handle it.

It's killing and extremely painful if you are an emotional person and have little control over your emotions. But you learn if you are willing to learn. Sometimes things come to an end and they are never the same again.

It pains because it is the end of something very beautiful. Something that money can't buy. For everything else, there is master card, they say.

"Peter finished his schooling in the Manipur and came to Delhi for his graduation. He rented a room near the University and hence started an important chapter in his life.

He was an excellent student in his state and scored over 90% marks in his 10+2 examinations and hence was admitted to a top college in the University of Delhi, one of the best universities in the country.

His father was a doctor in Manipur and had accepted his desire to go to the capital to further his studies. He chose a program in commerce (Honours) since there was an apparent demand for it at the end of the program in the job market. He had not taken up science because it did not interest him and hence could not become a doctor, which he knew would have pleased his father.

It was his first day in college and he went there in the best clothing he had with him. He knew he needed to buy some new clothes. 'I shall do that later, may be at the end of first week,' he reminded himself.

"Come here, chinki", a boy remarked, pointing towards him. 'Chinki' was the slang used to address people from north eastern states in Delhi, he learnt later. He also learnt that it was rather used contemptuously. The boy who called him was his senior and they wanted to rag him.

But as he was walking towards him, a teacher passed by and the boys ran away. He was saved from the trouble. He attended all the lectures scheduled and took his copy of the time table.

He made some acquaintances and met his classmates. He only liked one person out of all people he met that day.

"Hi, my name is Deepti, I am from west Delhi" she had said.

"My name is Peter and I am from Manipur."

Life went on. He was doing well in studies and also participated in many extracurricular activities. He would play the guitar that he had brought from Manipur with him and participate in inter-college competitions. He won many awards.

Since, he was popular, he made friends with many people and they would visit his room sometimes after the end of classes.

He realised one day that he had been thinking about Deepti very often and where had she been? Deepti seemed only interested in studies and nothing else.

She had round eyes, oval face and gleaming skin. She walked with grace and poise and everything about her was charming.

Peter decided that he will find a way out to talk to Deepti.

The next day, at the end of the class, he approached her.

"Hi Deepti"

"Hi Peter"

"How are you?"

"I am fine, thanks. How are you?"

"I am fine also."

"Deepti...would you...like to...share your notes with me?!" Peter had completely lost it. This was not what he had wanted to say. The exams were approaching and Deepti said that she had no problems in sharing her notes with him.

He took her notes home and smelled them all night.

Peter would call his home as often as he could, generally, a few times during the week. He told his father that there was no need to worry about the first year examinations and that he had prepared well. The exams lasted for a couple of weeks and Peter did not get any opportunity to talk to Deepti.

Deepti fared the best in the first year examinations. In fact, everyone had known how sincere she had been about studies and that was the only thing she was serious about. She did not seem to pay attention to anything else. She did have friends but they were also the studious and bookworm type people who had no other interest besides academic books.

Now, Peter had had enough and he was going to talk to Deepti this time.

It was the end of the last session on the first day after exams and he approached her.

"Hi Deepti"

"Hi Peter"

"Your notes were really helpful to me."

"You are welcome."

"Deepti, do you think you would have some time...to have coffee with me?"

"Well, ok. I need to leave for home now. Can we do another day?"

"Yes, yes, absolutely. Do you think Friday may be a good day for it?"

"Ok"

Deepti left. Peter could not contain his enthusiasm. He felt something happening inside his mind, sensations within his body- they told him that what he just did was very important to him and he was happy that he pulled it off. He had never asked anyone out for a coffee before and that is why, this was important to him.

This was Monday and 'the coffee meeting' was on the Friday. He felt that Friday is years ahead. He got restless and started praying that Friday should come as soon as possible. He attended the lectures but he was elsewhere in his mind. His eyes kept moving to Deepti over and over again. He moved them to the professor. They came back to Deepti.

Friday came. They had agreed to meet in a coffee house near their college after the classes. He reached first and waited- he believed this was a rule of courtesy for the boy to wait for the girl. She arrived 15 minutes late.

He smiled at her. She smiled at him.

He was wearing a black jacket and jeans. She was adorned beautifully in a salwar-suit in pink colour. She looked magnificent, he thought.

"Deepti, you look very nice."

"Thanks."

"I want to get know you, Deepti, if you will allow me."

"What would you like to know about me?"

"About your life, likes, dislikes, thoughts, dreams."

Deepti giggled. "I am a simple and a traditional girl from a conservative family. I do not think that much. What about you?"

They started talking and kept on talking. By the end of the meeting, they felt very comfortable with each other.

Peter was ecstatic and felt on top of the world. They started meeting often and even studying together. It was evident to each other that they were growing fond of each other and they did nothing to avoid the feeling.

Peter introduced Deepti to his friends and she started opening up and became more talkative. Peter also learnt to spend time with bookworms.

When they thought about each other, they felt that this was the most beautiful thing to happen to them.

When Peter thought about her, he felt that she was the prettiest creature on earth and nothing could have ever matched her beauty. He was so lucky to have her as a part of his life.

"Peter is such a wonderful person. I must be beautiful since he says so. I am so lucky to have him in my life,' thought Deepti.

Thoughts of future were consciously avoided. All they had wanted was to enjoy each other presence and love.

They did not even realize that the professor announced, "You will have your final year examinations next month and then your college life will be over. You will soon step into the real world. It will not be easy."

How did the time fly by?! Why was time always rushing?! What a heartless, cruel entity it is!

That evening, when they met, Peter sat in front of Deepti and stared at her. Within minutes, he had tears in his eyes. Deepti started crying also.

"I do not want to lose you, Deepti. Why did we never speak about it? *I love you.*"

This was the first time he had said this.

Deepti started crying even more violently. He hugged her. They kept crying in each others' arms for a long time. She sobbed, "I love you too Peter."

"I love you too."

"We will always be together," they consoled each other.

College life soon came to an end.

Both of them got jobs and started working. It made things difficult for them, as they were not being able to spend any time with each other. They decided that they will disclose their relationship to their families.

They did and here is what happened.

Deepti's parents were shocked. They could not believe that their daughter could have ever found a man for herself.

"How can I marry my daughter to a boy called Peter?!" her mother exclaimed and fainted! She had to be taken to hospital and administered blood glucose. She did not even take the time to express what she exactly felt about it.

"Deepti, we did not expect this!" her father said, confused about the appropriate behaviour in such a situation. Deepti did not say anything till her mother returned home. She had no idea what was happening.

One thing she knew was that she loved Peter and there was no conceivable reason in her mind why should she not get married to him.

She did not understand the reaction of her parents. What did her father mean by, 'we did not expect this.' What exactly did he expect? She had known that hers was a conservative family but she also knew that Peter was a great guy- intelligent, talented and most importantly, he loved and cared for her.

Nothing else was important in her mind. She wanted to make it work.

When her mother recovered and came back to her senses, the discussion resumed.

"What does he do?" her mother asked.

"He works with Infinity Dilbert Co Pvt. Ltd. in Marketing. We studied together."

"So that's what you studied. I see."

"Does he belong to our caste?" her father asked.

"Papa, I have no clue. I do not understand all this. I know I you would have liked to find a Panjabi boy for me. But then, I did not find one. I like Peter and he likes me. Isn't that enough for you? I will be happy with him."

Her parents looked very disappointed.

"This cannot be done. We will find another boy for you. Someone rich and who belongs to our caste and culture."

"No, please. Money is not the point. I want someone who takes care of me and someone I like and he is Peter" Deepti cried.

They had a long series of arguments. They tried to blackmail her in many ways. But somehow Deepti did not relent.

She was determined to succeed.

Eventually, her parents agreed to meet Peter. He spoke very respectfully to them because he had learnt to be respectable to elders and also because he was meeting Deepti's parents. The meeting meant a lot to him.

They had invited him over for dinner and it was his big opportunity to prove that he was the right boy for their daughter.

"What do your parents do?" asked Deepti's father of Peter.

"My father is a doctor in Manipur and my mother is a housewife."

"How long have you been in Delhi?"

"I came here for my graduation and now it has become home for me. I got a job after college and now I will live here. The job market in Delhi is better than it is in Manipur and since I could not become a Doctor, I cannot continue my father's practice in Manipur."

"Do you like Deepti?" Deepti's mother asked.

Deepti was looking at him at this point in time with dreams in her eyes. How badly she wanted this meeting to succeed! How badly had she wanted that Peter will be liked by her family.

"I like her more than anything else, aunty- more than anything I have ever liked. She means the world to me. I will do everything it takes to keep her happy. I know that as parents, you must have had a picture of a boy in your mind for Deepti. May be I do not look any close to that. But I assure you that I will do everything possible to keep her happy."

Deepti had tears in her eyes by now. She started sobbing. When girls do not know what to do, they cry. No one knew what to do. Poor peter, could not go and hold her!

The meeting ended every positively and Deepti's mother allowed her to go and drop Peter at the door.

Deepti could not describe the happiness. She looked at her parents' faces and sensed approval. She cried some more and hugged them.

Peter's family did not have objections. They felt grateful that Peter had found himself a wonderful girl and enriched their life also. Peter and Deepti would be married within a year.

End of story

Love

Some think that love is blind
Some think it just happens
Some think it is a decision
Some think it is hard to find

No matter what is true
It only happens to a select few
There is none who does not sense the feeling so high
The ones in love are those who do not let it die

We have one life to live, only one to love as well
One life to hold that hand, one life to feel that smell

One life to look in those eyes
One life to jump to those vibes

One life to sleep in the warmth of that lap
One life to get closer and kill that gap

One life to feel the blood rushing
One life to sense the heart hushing

One life to be with that special someone
One life that cannot be undone

One life to take that risk to say it all
One life to be everything or nothing at all
I wish everyone reading this gets to feel what they call love
This is life, this is it, and there is nothing so beautiful

<u>The Essence of Marriage</u>

There are too many trifles in life

And a few pivotal moments

Of all things, as men and women

We go through, whilst we survive,

The most important, the most sacred

Is the union of two lives!

Who decide to follow a common course?

Live the journey of life together

Through whatever comes their way,

Through pleasant or stormy weather!

Them seeking and with a promise of

Love, care and companionship

Now and hereafter, in our mind, heart and being

Not just ours, each others' lives we carry

This is really what happens,

When two people decide to marry

4.3 Being a loving Person

Be a loving human being- as much as you can be. All of us are emotional beings, no matter how hard we pretend to be. We are all tender and need love. We go around wearing masks telling the world that everything is hunky dory. Beyond the facade, everyone is craving for love.

I believe that a hug is a beautiful expression of love. Hug your friends. Hug your siblings. Hug your pet. Hug anything you can.

A hug

A Hug is an expression of love

It says a lot without a word

It says I am so happy to meet you

It says I like you

It says you are special to me

It says I miss you when you are not there

It says you and I need each other

It says that we are humans

It means many things at any time

Always touching, like the sound of a wind chime

A hug is a medicine

For apathy

For loneliness

For pain

So many people are recommended a drug

When what they actually need is a bear hug

A hug is a harmless act

All it does is build warmth, love and joy

I need a hug, do not tell me you do not need one

Give hugs, we all need some

In a society built with "who cares" as a seed

A hug is a joy that most of us need

4.4 <u>An Old Woman on the Street</u>

I saw an old woman today, alone, abandoned. She had a stick in her right hand and a small bag in her left. Her face was wrinkled and her eyes and body completely worn out. She was walking slowly, looking here and there so nobody hits her because she was just so frangible. Her hair was completely white and her body thin and weak. She looked left and she looked right. Her step could not be more than 4 inches at a time. She was wearing a faded dress, which bore complete semblance to her body.

I looked at her for 5 minutes while she moved slowly trying to save herself from the world she used to be an active part of, a few years back. She must have been a 16 year girl once upon a time in her life and boys would have fancied her. She may have been a mother for most of her life and nurtured and cared for children like us. She would have been a wife and had had a husband who may not be in this world anymore. She would have been a part of this world and then the world would have noticed her. I could do nothing to help her, to improve her life.

But today, she was alone, alone and scared. The world passed by and no one cared. Everyone was so busy and involved with their lives that they did not care to even notice her presence. She just does not exist anymore and nobody needs her.

I looked at her for 10 minutes and kept looking till she reached the end of the road and disappeared. My eyes were moist and they are moist even now at the thought of her.

Please do not let anyone meet the fate of that old woman; do not let our people ever feel that they do not exist…till they do!!!

5. Women

It is a Man's duty to woo a woman and the right of a Woman to be wooed

-Amar

For a long time, I thought about what to say. My views and feelings are so diverse about this particular topic that I am overwhelmed! Please bear with me, I have tried to understand this subject again and again and have been failing at exams.

I think that I respect women or at least I like to think so. You see, as men, we cannot live without them. I have read that science is in the process of proving that they can live without us!

Women hold this world intact.

They help men in maintaining their sanity or we will lose it. They are caregivers of this world. The mothers of this world bear children in their wombs. The sisters of this world do everything they can to see their brothers happy. The wives of this world await their men and care for them all their lives.

There must be exceptions. They do not dispute the rule.

Have you been able to understand ever the selfless love of your **mother**? Have you tried to understand why she sits by your side while you eat and just stares? Have you tried to understand why she calls you when you are out- multiple times? Why does she tend to think most of the time that you have grown frail?

I have tried to understand it. I think I have. But it does not make any rational sense to me. She does all this just to make sure that I am fine. Every small thing that bothers me becomes a project for her.

Let me give you an example.

Recently I lost a document- an insurance policy premium receipt. I badly wanted the document and kept looking all over the place but did not find it. My mother started looking for it after I was done. She asked me why, when, how about the document and looked visibly concerned about it. She also searched all over the house. She did not find it.

She asked me to search in a case all over. I had searched 5 times. I frisked it in front of her. I said it's not there and she said, "What's that small price of paper?"

I had not seen that paper earlier and it was the receipt. I did not express it but I was surprised at not being able to find it myself and her realising that it was there the first time.

She claimed all the credit for having found it, deservingly.

She does this all the time. Everything that bothers me a little bit bothers her even more. I know it. If something disturbs me and I tell her and she does not react swiftly, there is something wrong somewhere.

My mother is a woman. I love her.

***

Another important woman in my life is my sister.

Now, she does not talk as shamelessly as I do. She is a blessing to our small family and I am happy that we grew up in an environment where there was no discrimination for her. I would have felt ashamed of myself otherwise! In fact, I am happy that I have a sister. I know many people who don't know what it is like to have one.

By the way, I cannot prove it, but there may have been some discrimination against me!

***

Allow me to digress a bit. While writing this section, I have been confronted with a question-

"When does a girl become a Woman?"

It is similar to the question-

"When does a boy become a man?"

I addressed the former question by asking whoever I could ask in my small world...

"Are you a girl or a woman? Why do you think so?"

I will share the results with you in a while.

I addressed the second question by asking myself...

"Am I a boy or a man?"

I never cared to ask this question before. Interesting, isn't?

So, this is what I thought...

I am 28 years old. I can handle relationships and responsibility. I am an MBA. I have worked for over 4 years. So, does that make me a man? Why am I still not a boy?

Who defines it? What is the criterion?

If you consider the age for being eligible to vote, then I turned a man at 18 years of age. But...this does not make sense to me. I don't buy it.

So, did I become a man when I started working?

Well, okay, having a job does give you a certain level of responsibility but does that mean that there are no boys or girls working in companies? No. How about Business Process outsourcing companies. Most of them are young lads out of college or in college, speaking chic English. They definitely won't buy it. I don't, either.

Well, then, when you have a girlfriend, does that make you a man?

I don't think so. There are many emotional boys in foolish, childish immature relationships. So, I know they are boys since at one time, I was one.

Here is my answer. I have not taken this decision before and I am going to take it now. And I will tell you my reasons for it.

I am a man. I am not a boy anymore.

You become a man when you decide to be one.

You see, like anything else, it needs to be given considerable amount of thought at your personal level. You need to decide why you think you are a man and you are not a boy anymore.

Do not take anybody's rules. There is a lot of trash going around over and over in this world. People will tell you that you become a man when you are 25 years old or any stupid age number. Some will tell you that you become a man when you sleep with a woman or a girl for the first time.

Do you understand how ridiculous this is? In the world that we live in, many boys and girls are having sex in schools. I have no reason to believe that they are men/women who can handle the vicissitudes of life confidently. For that matter I know people who are double my age and cannot take it when life plays tough.

Here is my formula:

$$\text{Man} - \text{Boy} = \text{Perceived Maturity}$$

So, what I am saying that I think that I have a perception of maturity about maturity about myself. I decide it. No one else does it for me. I think I am a grown up and mature person who can handle difficult situations, handle responsibility.

What are the levels of Maturity?

- Physical
- Mental- logical and emotional
- Spiritual- A connect to the spirit within

Now, coming back to women or they will feel neglected. The question I asked was-

"When does a girl become a woman?"

Here are a few responses I received-

"A girl becomes a woman when she bears a child. That is, when she becomes a mother."

"I think I am a woman. I do not know when I stopped being a girl."

"I am a girl still for I do not have the maturity of a woman."

Look at the last response. It gives me my answer.

$$\text{Woman} - \text{Girl} = \text{Perceived Maturity}$$

Again, if you are a female, decide for yourself what you are. You decide for yourselves. It's a complicated question and needs cognitive effort. Exert it. It is more important than finding out what sub-sub-sub caste you belong to.

***

There are many things I do not like about the world I live in. One of those things is the way we treat women or girls, as a society. Things are changing for the better and that's quite a comfort.

There are women who feel that they should not have daughters! I cannot believe it. I heard a woman saying this a few days back- "God should not give the pain of daughters to anyone."

Many parents think it is a burden. So many young infant girls are killed in the womb.

Many men have no respect for their wives. They tend to think that once they are married to them, their wives are their property and liable to be treated roughly.

In our great capital city of Delhi, women are not safe on the streets. They are followed, harassed, scared almost every single day. May be it's not an important political issue!

I know all this sound trite because this is everyday news in the national papers- someone getting raped, molested, harassed and even burnt alive! Most of the perpetrators get away with these heinous crimes and life goes on! And all men get a bad name.

I do not live in an insulated world. It bothers me.

I remember one evening when there was chaos in New Delhi owing to the farmers' rally recently and I was crossing Janpath on foot with a female colleague. People were running here and there and we were scared running towards our car. One man came running to me and said, "Do not go that side. They are molesting women! My colleague in a fit of horror held my mind and we ran towards our car. We survived, thankfully."

She told me later that she was dead scared and that the greatest fear of a female is somebody harassing!

When I thought about it, it brings shivers to my body at the thought. I do not know how many shrieks are silenced and lives destroyed mercilessly, as I write this.

***

"Satender Singh and Preeto Kaur got married a year back. The couple lived in Ludhiana, Punjab, India.

Satender had a garment shop in Ludhiana city which his father had started after coming back from Pakistan. He had inherited the business. Satender's father did not work anymore and had retired from work 3 years back. His mother had been a housewife all her life. He did not have any siblings. He was told that when he was one year old, his mother gave birth to a boy who died within few months of birth due to pneumonia.

Satender had studied till class 12th, that is, he had about 14 years of school education. His parents had decided that this enough since eventually he has to come back to business itself, so there was no point in educating him much. He will learn the business by doing it after all and schooling was enough.

Preeto was a starry eyed, dainty girl. She belonged to a small family in Patiala. She was an undergraduate in English Literature. Her father worked in an engineering goods company and had a respectable monthly income. Her brother worked with an accountancy firm. He was not married as yet. Their family had decided that Preeto will get married first as the pressure is on the girls to marry first and similarly on the parents to marry their daughter as possible.

The pressure comes in various forms. It comes from relatives, from the society and friends. Everybody seems to be tense that someone's daughter is not getting married. God knows what is wrong!

We as a society have a long way to go in learning to mind our own business.

The marriage was arranged by a relative. She was an aunt of Preeto who had suggested the match. Preeto's father had been looking for a match for Preeto for over a year when this match came up.

The aunt had said, "Sardar jee, it is an excellent match for Preeto. You know they are a well settled business family in Ludhiana and have been living there for many years. You have no idea how much respect they command in the society there. Preeto will live like a queen for the rest of her life. You do not have to even think about anything."

The girl's family met the boy's family. Preeto met Satender for a few minutes during the meeting and thought that he was a simple man with simple values. Although she had her apprehensions about marrying someone who was less educated than her, her parents felt that it was a good match since Satender's family enjoyed a higher middle class financial status and Satender was tall and physically smart, the decision was made.

Satender's family demanded a bribe of Rupees 500000 (USD 10000), which would be duly paid by Preeto's father as this was a custom inbuilt in the society.

Not many people questioned the substratum of this custom. How did it make any sense whatsoever? Why should the girl's family pay any dowry? Are they buying the groom? People just accepted this as a part of life and moved on. Fathers of young girls worked all their lives to accumulate the dowry amount for their daughters and gave it away at the time of the marriage. Some people did not have the resources to pay dowry. Their daughters stayed at home or were abused by in-laws. In fact, one of the reasons daughters are still considered a burden by many couples is that they are financial liabilities!

The marriage was settled within two months as Satender's family members wanted. It was a frenetic period for both families and no one cared to ask what the rush was about! Preeto was married off and the entire community congratulated her father on having married off the daughter successfully (as if it meant good riddance).

Preeto had only spent about 3 hours broken down in a few meetings with Satender before they got married. It was not considered correct for the girl to ask to meet the guy before marriage and Satender had not asked.

When she had asked her father about it, he had said, "It is okay, Preeto, you have the whole life to spend with him and then you can understand him."

The dowry amount of Rupees Five hundred thousand was paid at the time of the dowry and the marriage was solemnised.

***

Preeto realised within the first week of marriage that she was going to have a rough time. She realised that she had married a man who did not have the intellectual capability to understand her. She wanted to work and she realised that Satender would not allow her to work. They did not have the opportunity to have this conversation earlier!

She was told by Satender's mother that she did not bring enough money with her. She did not understand this. Her father had paid what they had asked for.

She confronted Satender and complained to him about the comment made by his mother.

"What wrong has my mother said? You thought that you would just bring what my father asked for. What happens with 500,000 these days? You know when Ravi in our neighbourhood got married, his wide brought 200, 00, 00 with her."

"But that's what my father could have paid. He spent his life savings on the marriage also. How can you say all this?"

"That is none of my concern."

All that marriage meant to Satender was fulfilment of his sexual desire and the apparent social obligation.

Preeto felt distraught at her decision to marry Satender. In fact, she felt that she had been wronged by her parents also. They had given her no opportunity to talk to Satender. And now, she found herself in a mess.

When she became pregnant, Satender's family insisted that she should undergo an ultrasound to find out the gender of the baby in the womb. They wanted a boy. Preeto refused to undergo any test, at which she was abused and assaulted, until she gave in.

As luck would have it, the child was a girl.

All hell broke loose at the news.

Preeto's in-laws now insisted that she abort the child. She was horrified at their behaviour. There was no way she was going to take it. Although she had borne the harassment since her marriage, this was something that she was not going to take, come what may.

One of those days, Satender's aunt (his fathers' sister) came to see Preeto. She used to come sometimes as she lived in Ludhiana only. She used to like Preeto and understood her predicament but found her very helpless since she could not help Preeto. When Preeto disclosed to her what her in-laws were asking for, she was taken aback. She said that they are at it again.

"Preeto, I am going to tell you a secret that even Satender does not know. I think you should not take this at all. Save the life of your daughter and that of yourself. These people will destroy both lives.

Satender never had a brother. When he was a year old, another child was borne by his mother as they had wanted another son, but the child turned out to be a girl. These people have no respect for women whatsoever. The girl was thrown into the pond at the end of the city!"

Preeto started shivering. She called her father and told him to come to receive her. She did not tell him anything when he asked.

She told Satender that she was leaving forever and left with her father.

She filed a divorce application against Satender and the court granted her the verdict. Satender and his parents were sent to jail for 5 years.

Preeto took a job in Chandigarh and started a new life with the most adorable daughter in the world."

Sometimes she thinks about her decision of leaving her marital home and living alone. She was sure that she was better than what she would have been in a bad and painful relationship. And maybe she would find someone who would understand her."

End of story

SHE

She is a small girl making a twinkling sound
She is a young lady who makes the world go round

She is a wife committed to her man
She is a mother nursing all human

She takes many roles in this episode called life
If not for her, humanity would just not ripe

Respect her and honor her dignity
For her insult is appalling shame and boundless pity

You will never know if you do not let her survive
Your *gudiya* does deserve a shot at life

She is after all a human who makes a man complete
Let's give her the love, respect and honor
For she is in desperate need

6. Education and Work

"Education is what survives when what has been learnt has been forgotten"

-B F Skinner

Our education lays down the foundation on which we will build our lives and the work that we do occupies most of our time and since time is life, it occupies most of our life.

It is cardinally important, thus, to choose the kind of education we decide to pursue and the work that we will do. These decisions will have the most important impact on our lives than anything else.

How do we go about doing this?

By asking ourselves who we are essentially as human beings and how we can contribute to the world in our own way.

We can only contribute through what we have; the gifts that we have been bestowed upon us by the almighty powers- congenitally.

The purpose of education is help us understand this world through History, Geography, Mathematics, General Sciences, Social Sciences, Business Management, Economics or any subjects that we study in life.

After all, we will forget most of what we will study. What will stay or rather what should stay is ability- a cognitive ability to create our own world through the power of our minds. Education is our tool which prepares us to create a better world and that's where its role ends.

Work will occupy the majority of our lives. Work is what we do. Work, for most people is this world is who they are.

"What do you do?"

"I am a businessman"

"I am a Banker"

"I am a content writer"

“I am a model”

“I am a policeman”

“I am a doctor”

You see- *what you do, becomes who you are. It is that important.*

Let me tell you a story.

It's a story of 3 friends.

They graduated from the same business school and were picked up straight from the campus.

Their names were Sadhna, Samay and Saksham

Sadhna was a vivacious, bubbly and voluble girl from Delhi who believed in the power of her ambitions. She thought that she was quite a thinker and it was upon her to make something of her life. She did not think that women are made to weave sweaters all day and wait for their husbands to come back home! That was not her idea of a routine or life.

She wanted to succeed in whatever goals that she set for herself. She had worked very hard to enter the business school just like everyone else. In India, for many of the top institutes in any field of education, the success rate is less than 5%. The rest of the candidates have to compromise with mediocrity since they cannot manage to clear the entrance examinations and that as per the general perception proves their worth or worthlessness.

Sadhna's father was a business man. He was into the business of transportation of goods within the country and owned many trucks. So, financially she was not constrained and felt that in a way liberated her to follow what she really wanted to do. She did not have to take the loan since her father paid the entire fee. She had told her father that the fee was the last major expenditure he was incurring on her life and she would manage her life by herself henceforth.

Her father was very proud of her. He felt that she will become successful in whatever course she decides to pursue and he supported her in every way. Sadhna's mother was supportive as well, although fairly emotional as most mothers are. Sadhna prided herself on having the backing of an extremely supportive sense of parents.

She secured a distinction in the MBA program and participated in many co-curricular activities also. She was one of most popular students of the course and even the faculty had appreciative words for her.

Sadhna got a job with a construction and real estate company- CT Constructions Ltd. She was extremely elated at the offer since she had wanted to get into the real estate sector, among other choices that she was looking at.

CT construction was a 30 year old organisation based in New Delhi. They had evolved from being just a small construction company to an elaborate real estate company engaged in building of malls, organised residential units, commercial complexes and real estate consultancy services.

Sadhna had specialised in Marketing in her MBA. However she was picked up for a general management role. CT constructions was expanding its base to multiple geographies and going global. Sadhna will be responsible within a year to manage one of these projects. She would be working within a team and help grow the business of the company.

The first 6-8 months with the company would be solely dedicated to training her about the business, she was told. The company had picked up a team of 5 MBAs from different business schools and her peers in the group had specialised in different functional domains.

It was the third month of her training and she was enjoying herself.

She called Samay to ask him how was life at his end.

"Hi Samay"

"Hi Sadhna"

"How are you doing? How do you like the new job?"

Samay was born in Jaipur but his family had migrated to Delhi when he was 10 years old. It was in Delhi that he finished most of his education.

He had been a shy boy while he was growing up and did not change much till he finished his undergraduate college. He studied English Literature in his undergraduate program and worked briefly with a Public Relations firm before deciding that he will not be able to grow much in life without a sound post graduate qualification and so he decided to pursue an MBA.

The job in the PR firm made him confident about his creative and communication abilities and he started talking and expressing openly and almost effortlessly. He used to handle many clients who sought the services of the firm and this improved his confidence in dealing with people also.

Since he did not have Mathematics in college and was not very fond of it either, he faced a tough time cracking entrance examinations as most of them focussed on number crunching abilities. He finally made it and thought that it was a fluke and he could not do it in case he was to be asked to repeat his performance in the test which secured him admission to the institute. The group discussion and interview rounds were easy for him. He was very happy at securing admission.

The course was expensive and his parents had their doubts about prospects after the course. They consented after a lot of persuasion since they did not seemingly have a choice.

Samay's father was a serviceman. He worked with a multinational telecom services providing company as an engineer. Samay knew that his father would have liked him to be an engineer but he did not and studied literature. He had taken an education loan to pay half of the course fees. The other half was arranged by his father.

Samay's focus during the MBA program was to get a well rounded perspective on management. He laid tremendous focus on learning from his peers in the course since most of them were engineers and he thought that although he could not become an engineer, he respected them a lot. He was not as conspicuous as Sadhna during the program but successfully made his presence felt. He also wrote articles for the school magazine and helped in publishing it.

When the placement season began, Samay thought he will get into an organisation where he will get to work with people from diverse backgrounds and exercise his creativity in writing and expression.

He got selected in a logistics company. He did not understand how and why. All he remembered was that he had said something nice at the time of the interview to impress the panel and they decided that they will select him.

There were at least 50 people who had applied for a job in that company and he was the only one selected. He had no idea what they had found in him. He had had no interest in logistics whatsoever!

"What did they ask you? What did you answer? Tell us about it," his peers asked him after the interview.

"Well, they asked me why would like to join this company? I said that because it is a respected multi-national organisation in the supply chain business and starting my career with such a company would be a great start!"

"Excellent man, what else?"

"I told them that I am interested to learn about this business although my previous experience is in public relations. They said that they have structured training programs for people like me. Yes, it was a short interview after the selection test was over."

"Well done, Samay, we are all proud of you. We knew that you will do well. All the best to you" they congratulated him and life moved on.

The panel had commented that his attitude was very positive and they will be able to teach him the work. They needed people with the right attitude!

He had accepted the offer with a smile on his face, bewildered inside.

He had taken up the offer because he wanted a job and had the loan to pay.

"I am fine, Sadhna, trying to understand the logistics world. I make visits to shipping ports and understand how the shipping and logistic industry works. My company is a 3rd party logistics provider.

It is...interesting...in a way. We operate warehousing and transportation services also. Yes, basically, I am learning a lot of new things."

Sadhna could sense that Samay was trying to convince his own self and not her. She avoided asking any more questions.

"My training is going very well. It's a nice company. I may be moved to a new project at the end of the training period."

"Oh, that's very nice. I am happy that you are enjoying yourself. You have been a very confident person Sadhna and you deserve the best."

"Thanks Samay"

"Okay, listen. I have got to go now and will call you again soon. Bye"

"Bye."

Samay went into a contemplative mood after the discussion with Sadhna. He felt that Sadhna had got what she was looking for and he had been completely unlucky.

He should have waited for more companies and not just settled for any company that came his way. He had no idea about the logistics business. He was trying to convince himself every day that he found the job entertaining. He knew that he was lying to himself. He did not feel good talking to Sadhna at all. Somehow he felt that she would know what he was trying to hide and she did.

He had wanted to work in the media but no media companies had come to the campus. He had one of the best salary packages that were offered this time. His peers were jealous of him since many of them had wanted to work with that company and he was selected.

They did not get what they wanted. He got what he did not want, but a job.

***

Saksham was a quiet boy. He had an average built with an overflowing tummy growing from a sedentary life since he started working. He used to like playing cricket and football before he finished his college. When he thought about it, those times looked as if they were a century behind.

He grew up as a talkative child but somewhere during the course of his growing up years. He had had many friends in school. They used to find hard to keep him quiet. He would play many pranks and get away. He thought that life was wonderful when he was a young child.

He opted for Bachelor of Commerce (BCOM) for his undergraduate program in college. Since it was a general perception that BCOM is a program which does not need much intellectual rigor, his father insisted that he study for the Chartered Accountancy (CA) exams along with BCOM.

He cleared the initial tests but found that CA is too much for him to bear. He could not clear the intermediate papers and failed. His under graduation courses were also suffering along side. He thought that he will take the exams once again and will try to clear them but he could not make it again.

He attempted it 3 times but he could not succeed. He had heard horror stories of people who wasted years and years of their lives in trying to become chartered accountants and since they could not clear one level of the exams over and over again and had to give up, destroyed emotionally!

He wanted to get out of it now but he did not have the courage to face his father. He could not go and tell him that he will not be able to become a chartered accountant even after working so hard. He knew that his father would be furious and tell him stories of people who have been able to clear all the exams in the first attempt and how wonderful they were and how useless he was!

His graduation years had frittered away and he never really got time to grow up with his friends. The time was gone. Many of his college friends would go partying and invite him, but he could not go since he had his CA preparation. Even when he did not have classes, the guilt of having not been able to clear the examinations haunted him and he could not even think of going to a party. He started growing quieter and stayed to himself.

Even his friends in college felt bad for him but since he decided to be alone, they felt that there was nothing they could do! They wondered what had happened to Saksham. They tried to tell him to relax but he felt that pressure on him was too much to bear.

One evening, while sitting in his room, he thought of committing suicide! He felt that he could not take it anymore. There was no point in living life. He could not make anything of his life. BCOM would not lead him to any jobs. He could not become a CA. He had finished his graduation with second class since CA studies had taken most of his time. He was frustrated, disappointed and disillusioned with life.

He decided to give reality to his thought. This was something he could do. This will solve everything and put all the problems to rest. One day when his parents were out, he drank a bottle of a pesticide.

His parents returned home to find him unconscious on the floor with the bottle of the pesticide by his side! They rushed him to the hospital and he was operated. His parents were shocked and could not believe when the doctor told them that he drank the whole bottle and had attempted suicide!

He felt that it was unfortunate that he recovered.

He did not speak anything to anyone for a month. He had a see a psychiatrist, his family decided and the doctor arranged for one.

To his parents' respite, Saksham spoke. He told his story to the doctor and the reasons why he felt that he had to take such a step. He cried and sobbed.

The doctor told everything to his parents. They were only happy that he had survived the suicide bid. His father hugged him and said sorry for having created the kind of pressure that made him take this step. They decided that he will quit chartered accountancy.

Saksham slowly started recovering and coming back to his senses. His father did not stress him for anything anymore.

Saksham took up a job he was offered with a mutual funds company. His was a customer services profile. During the stint with the company, he learnt more about how mutual funds work and gained confidence about his ability to survive in the world.

He worked there for 3 years and then decided to go for MBA. He made it comfortably to the business school. He went on to specialise in Finance because that seemed to be the logical choice given his background.

Saksham was picked up by a bank and he was based in Bombay, although he had wanted to be in Delhi also as it was his home. He thought that he liked Delhi better and would have liked to be placed there. His family and friends were also there and that's where he had grown up.

The number of Banks and financial services companies was lesser this time on the campus owing to the financial slowdown. The sector had suffered from a tremendous fall in confidence due to the crisis.

He was hired in a wealth management profile for a multinational bank. As a part of his job, he dealt almost on every day basis with High Net worth Individuals (HNI). He was posted in Bombay. Bombay was the base of the Bank's operations being the commercial capital of the country.

He received a reasonable salary package and thankfully did not have a loan to pay since his father had paid for his education from his provident fund amount. This would eventually reduce the cumulative provident fund amount that his father would receive at on his retirement. It made Saksham guilty about his education and he felt that he must pay back the money to his father as soon as possible. He would.

He made calls to his clients or they approached him if they needed the services of a wealth manager. The world of financial services was extremely vast and complicated and he had spent many years in it already. He really liked it, he reminded himself.

One day, Saksham was working on a portfolio of a prospective client and he wondered- "What the hell! Why am I stuck here in the world of these numbers that I do not like? Is this what life is about? I do not think I enjoy this! I do not think I have ever enjoyed this. It started with chartered accountancy which led me to an MBA in finance and here I am, racking my brain on stocks, mutual funds, this investment, that investment! What the hell!"

He looked around at his colleagues. He suddenly decided that they looked like numbers to him- dry and lifeless. They did not have one characteristic of numbers- they did not change! Most of them had been with the bank for many years and had grown old with it. There seemed to be no whiff of energy in their faces. He wondered what his future held for him.

***

They had met in the library.

Samay had started the conversation. Sadhna joined in with her effervescence and Sakham was pulled along. It was the start of an important chapter in their lives.

The program was a roller coaster-at an electric pace. It had been tough and gruelling but had its exhilarating moments. Since the students got to spend time together with each other, studying day and night, partying and travelling, many of them got very close to each other. Everyone found friends who were like them. People seek congeniality, don't they?

The batch was an amalgamation of students from different parts of the country to become Masters of Business Administration (MBA)-one of the most popular educational programs globally.

They studied Marketing, Finance, Human Resources, Organization Behaviour, Leadership and many other high sounding subjects. They partied and laughed and cried together.

Isn't it a very important part of our education to teach us how to contribute to our environment, how to make friends, how to be a friend, how to survive in tough situations and survive adversity? They did not know it that these were some of the greatest lessons that they were taking home.

The level playing field allowed everyone to be themselves and those who could seize the opportunity made the most of it. At the end of the course, as is the nature of education, they had no idea how much do they remember.

After all, would that be applied in the real world? How much would they be able to use what they had studied? What if it is of no use?

For some of them, the question was...

Was it the right decision to go for the MBA?

***

Samay called Saksham.

"Hi Saksham"

"Hi Samay"

"How you been buddy? I have not heard from you for a long time. Is everything fine?"

"Yes, depends, what does everything mean?"

"I see...how is work?"

"You know I have decided something. I do not like financial services. I do not like finance. What the hell!

"Ha ha...what do you mean you do not like it? You have been in this field for years! Even before MBA, you were in the financial services sector! What happened?"

"You see Samay, that's been the blunder, all this while, all these years. When I could not clear the Chartered Accountancy exams, I should have realised why! I have no fascination for accountancy for financial services or anything. I have been doing okay professionally...alright, but that does not mean that I enjoy it! I don't. It's a pain to go to office and I hate getting up in the morning to see the sunrise. Why does someone not swallow the sun?"

"I see, you sound very tense Saksham. Relax. It will be okay. The good thing is that you have accepted and acknowledged this to yourself and now you can start thinking about what you can do about this problem."

"Yes, you are right Samay. Thanks. I will think about it but I am decided that I will have to move out of this rut as soon as possible and I want to come back to Delhi."

"Absolutely, come home, buddy. There are many people to welcome you here."

"How are you doing? And how is Sadhna? Do you guys meet?"

"I despise my work as much as you despise yours. I do not like the world of logistics. I am not saying that this is bad or unexciting, just that I do not think that I want to spend my life on dock yards and ships and tracking shipments and cargo and..."

"You also need to relax Samay."

"Yeah, I know. I have no idea what those people saw in me when they selected me. Of course I needed the job and that is exactly why I took it! I have the freaking loan to pay, which irritates me every minute! It's good you do not have the loan at least."

"Yes, it's good because there is no interest getting accumulated but I would like to pay my father as soon as possible. He borrowed money from his provident fund account for me."

"Yes, I know. By the way, Sadhna is doing very well. She is enjoying her training and she is in the sector that attracts her. She will be posted on any of the company's projects at the end of the training. CT is an excellent company, man. They take such good take of their employees and that is why everyone feels a sense of ownership and responsibility towards the company."

"True. Otherwise, these days it has become sheer platitude for many companies these days to say that the employees are their family when they treat them like bonded labour. I am happy for Sadhna too."

"Yeah"

"So, it's decided. I will find another job as soon as possible outside financial services sector. I think I will like working for a telecom company in sales. It's exciting how these technologies have changed our lives and it fascinates me. I will start looking."

"Yes, go ahead by all means and see if you can find a position that is based in Delhi. Life gets simpler at home. I will also get back to advertising and public relations. Let me call my previous company. They might have positions."

"Yes"

"Okay, Samay, I hope it's time we start making life-we will also make money, I am sure."

"So am I brother. I wish you all the best."

"I wish you too."

"Cheers to liberation."

"Ha ha...cheers to liberation."

Both of them started scouting for jobs which they felt that would do well in and where life will make better sense. Samay succeeded first and found a position in his previous company.

Sakham had to struggle for some time as he found difficulty in explaining to potential recruiters why he wanted to move out of the financial sector. But eventually, he managed to land a job in Delhi with Mantel Telecom Solutions.

He was delighted to come back to his home city and having come out of finance, once and for all, not too late in his life.

Sadhna hosted a party to celebrate the beginning of a new life for her closest friends. She could understand how good they felt and she was very happy for them.

They danced all night."

End of Story

7. Competition

I denounce the popularly accepted definition of competition around the world causing people to go mad. I have realised this after having going mad!

I am not competing with anyone out there. I am not trying to catch up with anyone. I compete with myself. Competition for me means to exceed the standards I set for my own self, to be a better person today than I was yesterday. If it's a race, it's my race with myself. There is no external competition.

-amar

I am about to finish writing this book in the times of the movie '3 idiots.' The hysteria around the movie has not died down yet and I hope it does not die for years. It is one of the most phenomenal movies our film industry has produced. Thanks to Aamir Khan and the teams involved in the making of these highly inspiring films.

I believe that human beings should not be compared to each other. No two human beings are same. The dynamics are just too complex for a comparison.

An orange can be compared with another orange. An apple can be compared with another apple. But we are not apples or oranges. Unfortunately, in the societal structure currently, people will compare anything possible.

They will compare a cow with a dog and say that dog is useless since you cannot milk it! Please allow me some exaggeration. I hope that the point is made.

Let's take an example. Roger Federer is one of the greatest tennis champions that world has ever seen. So was Pete Sampras. I used to follow Wimbledon quite vividly in Pete Sampras' times.

Now, who is a better player?

Who is supposed to decide?

What are the parameters of arriving at the decision?

Who can say that the parameters are sacrosanct and they cannot be challenged?

The experts of the game may say that the player who has one the maximum number of grand slam tournaments is the best. That is one parameter of success.

Now, someone else may challenge these criteria. One might say that that the player has won the maximum number of tournaments on grass is the best.

Someone else might say that no, clay is the right parameter of success.

According to all these different parameters, the result of 'the best' may be different.

What I am trying to say that 'the best' is a very subjective term. It depends on the thought pattern of the person who is deciding the parameters.

Your life is your race with yourself, not with anyone else. It's an everyday struggle and fight to be better then what you have been. It's a fight to be what you might be.

All competition with others is useless. We decide differently. We think differently. We compete differently. We work differently. The dynamics are not the same. They are different.

***

Let's take my writing as another example. The hypothesis is that 'amar is a good writer.' Now what happens?

Someone will say…'compared to whom?'

Whose writing would you compare this book to?

Let's think together of some parameters.

Who are the contemporary writers? What genre is this book in, by the way?

I have targeted this book to a young audience whose minds are still in the process of shaping up and who are not resistant to change like a lot of old folks who would regrettably say "I am too old to learn new things."

Now, who are the writers who are writing to a young audience? What kind of books have they written?

I will give you another great question. "What is the purpose of their writing?"

Let me give you **the purpose of my writing.** It may change, as I am always in a state of flux.

"I write to express life in a way I see it and more importantly, in the way I want to see it. I write to tell a story, a story that makes my readers think. I write because I love to."

Now, in order to compare me with another writer, you need to find someone who has had exactly the same purpose. Isn't?

May be you can find someone who has a similar purpose. But I doubt you can find someone who had the same purpose exactly.

Then, you can start comparing. There will never be a justifiable comparison.

I have read many books and written literature in my short life so far. I will continue to read because I cannot live without it.

Have there been writers who have influenced me?

Yes, absolutely. There are many. If I need to pick up one writer who has had the most influence on my thinking, she was Ayn Rand. I love her writing, almost every sentence of it. You can say that amar as a writer is influenced by Ayn Rand's work.

I think that may be correct. So far, I have read *the Fountainhead* and I am reading *Atlas Shrugged*. I am sure that if I stay alive for some more time, I will read every word of her work.

But then you cannot compare. If I reach even a few percentage points of the quality of her work, I will feel proud of myself. To me, Ayn Rand was God.

I am not competing with anyone. I am working on being a better writer with every page I write. I am competing with myself.

Do not insult yourself by comparing yourself to anyone else. You are unique. You are unprecedented. There have been people before who have looked like you, spoke like you, had other similarities, but no one was exactly the same. Even identical twins have a difference in their fingerprints, that is, besides their thoughts.

-amar

"Aditya Gupta was an average student. He belonged to a lower middle class income family in India. His parents thought that he was useless. They would always compare him to his sister who was a topper in her class. They would also compare him to his cousins, his neighbours, anybody they could think of. Everyone was better than Aditya. It was tough for the poor boy to keep him motivated for anything with only discouragement coming his way at home.

He did not find much interest in studies. Passing the exams was only a measure to please his parents and relatives to him. He spent as little time on studies as possible as was required to pass examinations.

He liked cricket and was the Captain of the college cricket team. Nobody cared about that in his family.

He was doing BA in English from a college in Delhi University. He got admission there because of his cricketing genius. He had been leading his school cricket team also.

On the basis of his marks, he would not get admission to a regular course in Delhi University. These days' marks were touching sky high and one could not think about admission in any college of the University of Delhi with less than 80% aggregate marks. The top colleges had cut offs in the range of 90-95%. The times were not far when there will be students with 99% marks and they will be told to stay out since there would be students with 100% marks in their school leaving examinations.

Aditya had scored 72%!

The entire neighbourhood was tense about it.

Mrs. Verma who did not have anything to do than sitting outside her house and staring at people had come to visit Aditya's home after she heard about the news.

"What will Aditya do now? You know these are the times of intense competition and I have no idea what will happen of him now. With these marks he will not get admission anywhere. You know Mrs Sharma's son Sameer scored 75% last year and he could not get admission anywhere. He is now in Pune working at a cycle repair shop. What could he have done! These are tough times. What will happen of Aditya now?" she said this to Aditya's mother, Mrs. Gupta.

"We do not know. I think he will do something. We have not decided as yet. Let us see."

"Ok. Do not worry, please. I do not know what is happening to the world these days. Oh, my God, these are tough times." Mrs. Verma left with these words; seemingly disappointed.

Everyday should would sit outside her house and stare at everyone. No one understood what her purpose was and what drove her.

That night, Mrs Gupta and complained to Mr. Gupta.

"Mrs. Verma had come and said that there is no hope for Aditya. You know, Sameer, who scored 75% last year did not get admission anywhere and now he works in a cycle repair shop. I wonder if our Aditya will go the same way."

Aditya's father got very depressed about it. He did not say much at that point in time and went out for a walk.

Aditya was so relieved after getting admission into the full time college. He wondered what would have happened in case he did not. So many people were dying of heart attacks these days! Thanks to Cricket, he could survive in this world.

Aditya's father had a small business. He used to manufacture certain equipment used in the water meter and supply it to the meter manufacturing companies. There were many such companies in the market. The market was big by that measure but since there were other manufacturers of the same equipment, there was competition and the margins were going down.

His father would talk to his mother sometimes about the ills facing his business and how life is becoming even more difficult with every passing day.

The family had a small house with 2 rooms and a kitchen and since the house was small, Aditya could generally overhear whatever his father was saying. He did not know if his father wanted him to overhear all that. He felt that he did.

Unfortunately for his parents, Aditya had no interest in the business. It did not make any sense to him, like most things. He wondered how could spend all his life making an equipment that gets fitted in a water meter. Is that all there to life?!

"I want to be a cricketer," he told himself. He did not think much about it, but he was also very good at writing in English. He did write a few articles in the school magazine, but since no one appreciated, his interest drifted away. But he did not get away from cricket since he felt passionate about it.

Aditya's sister was an ace student. Her name was Ashna. She was in standard 12th and brilliant in BPCM- biology, physics, chemistry and mathematics. She wanted to become a doctor and all signs for it were positive.

Throughout her student life she had been a topper in her school and had received many academic awards. Students from the neighbourhood would come to visit her with their doubts and she would help them out with a touch of modesty.

Aditya and Ashna had a nice, friendly, brother-sister relationship. Aditya was the elder brother and he felt a bit inferior to his sister inside, although he never mentioned that. He knew that she was such a star student and everyone eulogised her for her academic prowess.

One day, he asked her to accompany her for a walk.

"How are you so intelligent Ashna and I do not have the same interest or intelligence?" he asked her.

"Well, I do not know Adi. I just like it. In fact, I do not even spend as much time studying as some of my friends do. It comes naturally to me, I believe. People get surprised at the way I solve problems in mathematics and physics and I am surprised at their getting surprised about it!

I wonder how you do not understand it. Have you exerted enough effort?"

"But I have Ashna. I do not get it. You know these science subjects that you study completely do not enter my mind. I almost flunked in physics while in standard 10th. In case I did not get rid of them then, my life and personality would have been completely destroyed by now. Not that I have made much of myself, but I am happy I chose arts.

I am studying English now and I like it. I enjoy reading literature. There is so much wonderful literature written in this world by writers in many genres and I enjoy reading it.

I love playing cricket and am the Captain of the cricket team, although no one cares about it at home. I scored a century in the last inter college tournament and there are murmurs around that some of the players from our college may be given a chance in the state team."

"Do you think you will be able to spend your life reading literature or playing cricket, Adi? You know how tense are mummy and papa about your future? Mrs. Verma came yesterday also and said all sort of stupid things."Ashna asked, conspicuously worried.

"I cannot say anything for certain right now, sister. I am working hard on cricket and that is my hope right now. If I do not succeed in cricket, perhaps I will try to become a journalist since I am a good writer.

"Somebody should have a place for me in this wide world!"

"I *hope* so." Ashna said, looking into Aditya's eyes.

People got busy with life. Mrs. Verma also forgot about Aditya's studies and focussed on other people.

Aditya's fathers' business improved. Ashna topped the pre-board examinations in school. Her school leaving examinations would be held within 3 months and everybody knew that she would sweep the exams to become as the state topper or may be the national topper. She was also preparing simultaneously for medical entrance examinations that she would need to crack to enter a medical college.

Aditya was now in the second year of his under-graduate program. The exams would be held within 2 months and the selection for state level cricketing tournament was to be done within a month.

He did not discuss the issue with anyone at home, although he had briefly spoken to his sister sometime back about it. This time, he did not tell anyone about the dates.

He really wanted to make it to the state team. There were 4 spots in the state team and he was one of the contenders. There were 16 contenders. He had to work really hard and prove his mettle in order to be selected.

The selection, it had been declared would be based upon performance in the 2 week inter college tournament to be held at the end of the month.

Aditya felt that his life depended on it. He decided that he would devote all his attention to cricket for now and in case he did not get selected, he will give up cricket and start focussing on his undergraduate studies.

It was a risk he decided to take. He decided it was going to be a boundary or nothing. It will not be a single.

He started working on it all day. He would leave home in the morning and come at the end of the day. His mother asked once, "You are coming unusually late these days, any reasons?"

"I go to my friend's place to study. We are preparing for the exams. I want to score better this time."

His mother looked extremely surprised and walked away.

He would get up early in the morning and reach college. The coach was available from 630 am to 830 am.

"You are doing well Aditya. But as the Captain of our college's team, if you win the tournament for the college, the chances of your selection will increase. You have got to understand that you will have to perform not just as active member of the team but also as the Captain to make it to the state team." Aditya's coach reminded him.

"Yes, Sir, I understand."

"In case you make it, do not forget me."

"No chance of that, Sir."

The competition will be tough, everyone was heard as saying. There was excitement in the university about the inter-college tournament.

Aditya worked every moment he could. He could only do something about his effort and nothing about what others were doing. He motivated his team everyday and drilled into their mind that they are going to be the ones who will pick the crown. He focussed on his batting since that was his area of strength and worked extensively on fielding. He was fighting against himself everyday in nets and making sure that he did everything possible to win.

8 colleges were participating in the tournament representing a team. The selection for the state team was to be made by a special committee appointed by the University out of the 16 contenders.

Group A	Group B
Team A	Team G
Team B	Team H
Team C	Team I
Team D	Team J

Every team in group A will play a match with the opposite team in Group B, as shown in the table. The matches would be played in knock-out format in this round.

Aditya's college represented team D in group A. Their first match was with Team J.

The tournament started with tremendous enthusiasm. Cricket is informally the national game of India.

It was a strong match. Team J batted first and scored 275 runs in playing first. Aditya scored 85 and took 3 catches.

Aditya's team won by 6 wickets and entered the semi finals. Aditya was applauded by his team and coach for the victory. There were students from around the university to watch the matches and buzz was exhilarating.

At the end of round I, 4 teams were left in the tournament:-

Team G

Team H

Team C

Team D

The structure of the semi finals was as follows:

| Team G | Team D |
| Team H | Team C |

Two games were all that it would take to decide the course of his destiny. He wanted it badly. He could not afford to fail.

In the semi final match against team G, he managed to score 49 runs. They batted first and the total score in 50 over was 225. Team G had some excellent bowlers and they did not allow the otherwise rampaging players of team D to hit many boundaries.

This was a tough total to defend. He confronted his team and told them, "225 is a decent score and we will defend it. We will defend it because we will not allow them to hit any boundaries. If they do, we will not allow the ball to hit the boundary line, we will jump and stop everything. We will win. This day will not return. Fight your guts out."

Team D was a different team that day. They turned into a bunch of flying men who did not allow the ball to cross the boundary. The bowlers were at their best. These were men on fire.

Team G managed only 187 runs.

Aditya and his team were off into the finals.

He could not contain himself. His family had not known about the tournament so far. He did not think that it was of interest to them till he won!

Aditya's coach decided to invite his family for the final match secretly.

He went to house and told them the story. Aditya had no idea that his family had been invited.

The final match was between team D and team H. The stadium was mad with excitement. Students from all over the university thronged to watch the final match.

Aditya faced his team. They were looking at him for words that have had been pushing them to perform at their best.

Aditya said, "My friends, you have made it to the finals. You are all stars. Today is a very important day in your life. Go and make the most of it."

The teams arrived in the stadium to a big applause, waiving to the spectators.

Aditya was looking towards his right while walking towards the stadium when he saw his father, mother and sister. They were all clapping. He stood struck as if by lightning. He did not move for 5 minutes. He could not believe his eyes. His father moved his hand over his head and said, "All the best, my son."

Ashna held his hand and said "all the best bhaiya (elder brother)." His mother just kissed on his forehead.

He could have asked for nothing more on perhaps the most important day of his life so far.

He started walking towards the stadium and looked backwards on the left and saw his coach just gestured the sign of victory. Aditya was on fire. They won the toss and decided to bat.

He had been opening throughout the tournament. He hit the ball all around the place and scored a century. He raised the bat and gestured towards his family.

The team scored 309 runs.

Team H gave a good fight. At one time, it looked that they will achieve the target. They were running at a run rate of 8 runs per over till 20 overs, when Aditya took an incredible catch to claim the wicket of their lead tournament. Team H managed to score 300 runs and team D won the tournament.

The stadium exploded. It was a great final match to watch.

Aditya was adjudged the player and the captain of the tournament.

His father said, "Aditya, I am proud to have a son like you. I am sorry for not realising your worth and wanting to fit you according to my expectations. I have realised my mistake and so has your mother. I am sure your sister is extremely proud to have you as her brother. Well done."

His college decided to allow him another month to prepare the exams.

His coach arrived with an envelope after a week of the end of the tournament. Aditya could not stop himself from the excitement of positive expectation.

There was news that he was dying to listen to. The coach told his father, "Aditya is one of the 4 players who have been selected for the state cricket team. Congratulations to you, Aditya."

A new life awaited Aditya where he was king of his own destiny. He won.

Mrs. Verma came to see the Guptas when she heard that Aditya had been selected in the state team and exclaimed, "Oh, Aditya I always knew that you were an excellent cricketer and a very talented boy. I knew that you will make big in life one day and you have done it."

 Aditya chuckled and thanked Mrs. Verma.

End of story

Follow your own destiny. You are the one who will live it.

-amar

Of course this story was imagination. But I believe that there are so many 'Aditya' in the world we live in.

I think it is critical for us to understand how we are going to compete in this world and create a place for ourselves.

Comparison is a constant pain in our societal structure. If you are student, your parents compare you to your peers. If you are an employee, your boss compares you to your colleagues-all the time. This sort of culture has immense potential to destroy self esteem and many lives. It is happening every day.

Do not take my definition if you do not like it. I have attempted to present my point of view. Create your definition. Feel good about yourself. There are many morons around whose only job is to steal your confidence and that's all they do. Do not let them.

For your own sake, be yourself! It's your life. It's your respect and dignity and they are worth more than anything else in this world.

8. Adversity

Life isn't all sunshine and rainbows- it's a very mean and nasty place out there and I don't care how strong you are- it will beat you down to your knees and keep you there permanently if you let it. You mean a no-body. It is not about how hard you hit, it's about how hard you can get hit and keep moving forward, how much you can take and keep moving forward- that's how winning is done!

-Rocky Balboa

A few are tested and a fewer survive. The rest just fritter away

-Amar

I am amazed at the fortitude of certain people around me. I will give you one example.

I happen to know an old man who lives with his old wife. I cannot tell you how much I admire his strength. I have no words for it since I do not understand his motivation. I have thought about it many times. I have no idea what keeps him going. I do not know what drives him to get up every morning from the bed. I think that some people's sheer existence is an inspiration in itself. To me, he is one of them.

He had 3 grown up sons. He does not have any now. It wasn't the old man's fault. He raised them so they would be there till his last days and now there is none.

The other day he was having his regular walk in the park while I was working out. I greeted him and asked him about his well being.

He replied, "All is well, thanks to God's grace."

I felt like giving him a salute.

In contrast, I am surprised at the way other people give in to difficulties.

People lose their mental balance, commit suicide or just become irrelevant. So many people just lose the will to carry forward and in fact they die that day.

The mind is its own place, and in itself, can make heaven of Hell, and a hell of Heaven

-John Milton

Life is tough. It is difficult to manage its vicissitudes and maintain a sense of calm and balance. It is tough to keep going at times. Absolutely, it is. There have been so many times in my life when I felt that the best thing to do is to sleep forever and never get up.

But we are human beings-the most powerful creatures on earth. Just look around you, you will find people who are handling extremely painful situations with imperturbability that is almost fascinating!

You will be hit. Something will hit you from the blue just when you think you have got it all settled! Now, you can stay down or you can get up and start again.

Yes, start again. We will be required to do this multiple times in our lives if we want to live lives that amount to anything! We will be required to put things at stake and run the risk of losing.

***

Businessmen are great people. To my mind, business is the most productive force mankind has discovered. It has changed our lives positively for generations and it continues to do so as I write these words. But all that looks rosy isn't so. A vast majority of business attempts fail. You know what that means? That means efforts, money, jobs going down the drain! It can be distressing. It can be disastrous for someone who has taken a bank loan to find his business and has his personal property attached as collateral. Is it adversity? Absolutely it is.

Some of the greatest businessmen have failed many times. They picked up what they learnt and started again.

""Failure is the opportunity to begin again more intelligently."*

Henry Ford

It is extremely important to learn how to deal with failure. Rather, it is even more critical to understand what failure means to you.

To my mind, there is only one form of failure. It is in giving up the fight. If you have not given up, you are not a failure

- Amar

You may be facing a setback. This means that something has happened that had stalled progress *temporarily*. It is temporary and just for the time being. If you decide that it is the end of your life, it will be. You are, after all, what you think.

Setbacks are just one form taken by adversity.

People die.

It is extremely tough to handle the death of loved ones! Hell! I think it is the toughest thing in the world. But then, people die! There is no way we can prevent it and it requires tremendous emotional strength to tell you that there is work to be done.

Breaking up of a relationship which started with a foundation of blissful love?

Absolutely, it hurts like needles all over. When someone you deeply love, leaves you, your entire emotional world comes tumbling down and you wonder how would you pick it up again? Well, you cannot stop anyone from leaving you as you cannot force anyone to love you either.

Things happen and people change for whatever reasons of theirs and relationships come to an end. They do and they will. You will find someone better if you keep looking, someday.

How about losing your job?

Ask me. I just lost it for no fault of mine. Someone asked me the other day, "Oh my God, you lost your job! What will happen now?" as if it was the end of the world.

"I will find another one." I answered and the gentleman walked away, I think disappointed with my answer.

All or any of these happenings do constitute adversity. No one wants to encounter it but nobody is insulated from it. It will hit you sometime or the other, in one of the other way.

The important thing is that you accept what has happened. Get up and start walking again. Don't stay there and do not expect people to come and pick you up. Nothing will happen. You are responsible for yourselves.

You are the one who will have to pick up the pieces and start all over. Make a gratitude list and say thanks for everything you have. Say thanks for your health, your education for being able to read these words, for people who love you, for people who need you, for all the wonderful reasons you have to be thankful for.

Start again because you have the blessing of being alive, if nothing else. If you don't, you will fritter away and the world will move on.

Think about it. Do you think the world cares? When someone dies, it just moves on. And that is the right thing to do. Many great men and women who have been a part of the human civilization have passed away.

You will, too. I will, too. While we are here, let's make the most of it. Let's be of use and have a whole lot of fun!

Don't ever quit, no matter what the circumstances.

Fight on. Stay strong.

***

Nischay was born in a slum in Delhi- a dirty, squalid place. His father was a cobbler. His mother died at the time of giving him birth.

His father would drink a lot. Till he was 5, he spent a lot of time with his aunt (his mother's sister when his father would go to work. Then, he started accompanying his father to work as well.

He started to learn how to mend shoes. He would get up in the morning at 6 and accompany his father to work and work till about 8 in the evening. They could not afford food otherwise. He and his father would together make about 150 rupees a month. They would work at a corner of a building which had many offices. So, they would sit there and await customers who would need polishing, mending and repairs.

They lived in small room in the slum. It was in a dilapidated state and used to stink and that was the world as Nischay had known. There were no basic facilities like electricity and sanitation and the place was home to diseases. Nischay had encountered Malaria while he was 3 years old and took months to recover. He was treated in a government hospital. The state of the hospitals was pitiable. Thankfully, he had survived. A lot depends on God's mercy in such an environment.

This name was given to him by his aunt. He liked his name, although he did not know what that means. It meant 'resolve,' as thought by his aunt. She loved him and did not want him to lead a mean and filthy life that the slum guaranteed.

He was 10 years old and he had learnt the entire job profile of a cobbler. Till now, he had had no access to education. His aunt had pleaded with his father to send him to school but he had not relented. His father wanted him to work and bring some money so they could afford food and some liquor.

One day, he was polishing shoes for a man who owned a shoe manufacturing facility and asked him about his life. Nischay told him that he had learnt this job from his father and that he knew nothing else.

The gentleman felt bad for Nischay and wanted to help him in some way or the other. He asked him if he could meet his father.

The gentleman's name was Nirnay which means 'decision' and he thought if this was one of the reasons that he liked Nischay.

Mr. Nirnay met Nischay's father to explain the offer he wanted to make to his son.

"I would like to offer a job to Nischay in my factory in the evening for 4 hours a day. During the day he can go to school. I really want to see him going to school."

"But why would you want something like that?" Nischay's father retorted.

"Well, I know what it means to be a child without education. I never went to school all my life and whatever I learnt, I learnt it from life. It pains me to see another child going without education. You may say that there are thousands of children like Nischay all over the country. That is correct, but I like Nischay, I am not exactly sure why.

Please allow me to help me. It will perhaps be the redemption of whatever wrong I have done in my life. He will work. I will pay him a salary and his school fees also."

"I will think about it."

"Please do. This is my card. Give me a call and I will tell you when to send Nischay to my office."

Nischay wanted to study. He had seen school going children while he was going to work and he felt how and why he was different. He did not have any answers. He was told that he was just unlucky that he was born in a poor family and his father could not afford to send him to school. Like many children in India, he was supposed to work to earn a living.

He had requested his father one morning to send him to school. He was told to stay quiet and go to work. He did so and dismissed the idea.

Now, he felt hope. He did not say anything to his father since he did not want to face his wrath. He did not understand why Nirnay wanted to help him to go to school. All that he understood was that he had a chance.

He will have to work very hard to go to school in the morning and work in the evening. But he wanted to do so.

It took a week for his father to make a decision. His aunt played a major role in convincing him that it was completely a win-win situation for him and Mr. Nirnay was just a Samaritan who understood Nischay's predicament.

Finally it was decided that Nischay would go to school. His father accompanies him to Mr. Nirnay's office and salary was decided. As agreed, Mr. Nirnay would also pay Nischay's school fee.

It was the beginning of a new life for Nischay. He was about to turn 11 within a month and he was joining school. He was told by his aunt that he must study hard as they are the means for him to walk out of this dirty world.

Nischay started to learn alphabets and numbers in the morning and make shoes in the evening. His day would start at 0530 am and end at 2300 hours. He worked hard as he realised that he will have to make up for the lost years. He learnt fast. His teachers appreciated him.

In one parent-teacher meeting, Nischay's mathematics teacher applauded him in front of his father.

"You son is excellent at Mathematics. He is so fast that he does calculations so fast that he makes others feel slow about their speed. We may be able to push him up by a couple of classes."

"Thank...thank you Madam" Nischay's father said with folded hands. He felt proud of his son and kissed him. He thanked Nischay's aunt for convincing him to send him to school.

***

Nischay's aunt had been the mother to him that he never had. She did not have any kids herself. That was one reason she loved Nischay so much. Her husband used to sell vegetables and they were poor family like all families in the slum. She could not bear any children and so her relationship with her husband was a formality not well attended to.

He did not talk to her and would not come home for days. She would not even know whether he was dead or alive during those days. She managed her expenditure by sewing clothes for ladies in the neighbourhood residential society as her husband did not pay her anything.

She wanted to see Nischay succeed. When her sister died, she had held her hand and told herself that she would do whatever she could do to ensure Nischay's well being. When Nischay started going to school, she was extremely happy. She would sit with him sometimes to see his books and would find time to learn something herself so she could teach Nischay if he needed help.

***

Mr. Nirnay would often visit Nischay in the factory to ask him how things were. Sometimes he would also visit his father and aunt in the slum. He had had a tough life himself.

He was the son of a school teacher. His mother was a housewife. When he was 6, his father had an almost fatal accident which crippled him. Since his father had been the single earning member of the family, there was no one now to bring money home.

He had to pull out of school and begin working. He had started by doing odd jobs like distributing newspapers and selling cooked food which his mother would make. He did so for many years.

By the time he was 21 years of age; he had worked at many jobs and learnt life on the street. He got interested in manufacturing shoes during one such job where he had worked in a shoe design unit which provided design consulting to shoe manufacturers. He felt that there was a good profit to be made if costs were kept low.

He had learnt by observing and listening to conversations.

He decided to start a small operation in a shop he rented where he hired some men and began to teach them the designs. He managed to keep his costs manageable and his business acumen turned him into a profitable businessman.

He had never employed a child in his factory before. He employed Nischay for the sole purpose of making sure that another childhood is not wasted like his. He wanted to make a real difference to Nischay's life and felt delighted to see him progressing.

***

Nischay progressed brilliantly. Now his father's mission was to make sure that Nischay finished his education. He would work from day to night to make sure that he earned money enough to support his son in any way possible. He stopped drinking completely 2 years after Nischay started going to school.

Nischay finished his schooling with flying colours a few years down the line.

He went to college to study engineering. He got selected in the best engineering college in the country. His classmates are fascinated by his story and life. He rose from slums and had to work double as hard to make something of his life. His father was a cobbler and a drunkard. He never had a mother. He was mothered by his aunt.

Had a stranger from the blue not been kind to him, he may have been still sitting under a tree mending shoes.

Nischay knows that he can handle anything that comes his way. If he could bear and go through what he has already seen in life, there could not be anything that is hard for him. If he is hit, he will rise and not be stopped.

He is the inspiration for everyone who knows him. He makes their struggles melt at his sight.

STAY STRONG. FIGHT ON

Stay strong, fight on
Very soon you will see light
Not yet, don't give up the fight!

Sometimes life tries you left, right and centre
Everything seems to fall, all over
The test is of your endurance, of will, of your power to hold on
Do not give in, it is momentary, things will change in not so long

So hold on, press on
You have faced tough times before,
Hold on to see how things will change anew
They say it over and over
Tough times don't last, but tough people do

So hold your chin high and smile like you always do
If anyone can make it, if anyone can change it, if it all rests on anyone, it's YOU
I do not believe in GOD, but the almighty powers sure have a plan,
The Alchemist said that the darkest hour of the night comes just before the dawn

The dawn will come; it will be a lot of fun
Wonderful people, wonderful places, a wonderful life embrace those
Who, in the face of a ferocious battle
Battle it out and not run

It will all change, take my word
I am sure I am not wrong
You have only yourselves to fear

Stay strong, Fight on

9. Retirement

Life is a battlefield, die fighting

-amar

I do not understand retirement from work. I do not think anybody should retire from work. There should be only one form of retirement- from life, which is anyways, compulsory.

From the perspective of business, it makes sense for companies to let young people take over responsibilities when people retire from companies. Young people bring new ideas and new initiatives to the table which makes the business grow in new directions.

However, as individuals, it is important for us to realise that we are born to work. That's the most important thing about life.

Many successful businessmen do not want to retire since they were the ones who founded the business and the business is them. Richard Branson, the founder of the Virgin Group, has mentioned in his autobiography that he enjoys what he does so much that the thought of retirement does not attract him.

Mr. Venkataswamy or Dr. V, as he was universally known started Aravind Eye care system at the age of 58. He died at the age of 87 and his legacy continues. Aravind is the one of the largest and most productive eye care facility in the world.

Ray Kroc pioneered the McDonalds concept at 52.

Khushwant Singh wrote well into his nineties.

Gritty and determined people have proved over and over again that age is just another number.

Do not let age stop you from achieving from dreams. It's never too late. You are only as old as you think you are.

-amar

Let me tell you a story.

Rakesh Batra retired from work at the age of 60. A valediction was given in his honour by the head of his department and he was garlanded and complimented. Everyone wished him a healthy and happy retired life.

"Rakesh, you have worked very hard for all your adult life. This is the time to relax and enjoy. Please do not get stressed at all. Remember, as they say in Hindi...

Chinta Chita saman (Anxiety is like pyre)

And anytime you wish to come back to the office to say hi to us, please do. We will all welcome you with open arms. After all, this is your office. All the best!

This was the beginning of a new chapter in Rakesh life. He felt that this would be the last. He had married off his two kids. One lived in Bangalore and the other one lived in the United States of America. They had their own families. He had been waiting to retire for the last few years. He thought that he had already achieved everything that he was supposed to achieve and what more was there to life!

In his neighbourhood itself, there were a few men who had retired and now spent time at home. This is what most people do. They spend time with their likes talking about politics and cursing the leaders, eating, sleeping and travelling. This is what he will do also.

He had been a clerk for most of his life in a government department and had a menial job, in his own view. He lived to make sure that his kids got good education and that his family was well fed. That was something he managed to ensure with his job. A job is meant to provide for the family, after all. He did not ever think about having a purpose in life. Most people live purposelessly after all, he thought. This talk about a life of purpose was all mumbo jumbo.

His kids were doing well for themselves. His son was a software engineer working for a multinational corporation based in Seattle. He was married and had a son. So, he had seen his grandson, which was quite an achievement. His daughter worked as an English teacher is Bangalore. The family had decided that teaching was the best profession for a girl since it allows her to manage work and family very well and that is why she was made to go for B.Ed. (Bachelor of Education) after finishing her schooling. She was married to an engineer also. They had a daughter. It was an achievement, again.

When people die, their life should be measured by the yardstick of how many generations they have been able to see, seemed to be the general consensus implicitly arrived at.

So, now, he was retired. It was his first day, having retired yesterday. His son and daughter had called in yesterday to congratulate him on the culmination of his working career.

His wife looked curiously at him and smiled, as she served him tea.

"Mr. Batra, so what do you plan to do now?"

Mrs. Batra had been a housewife and had taken good care of the household. She was a graduate but never felt any inclination to work. She was happy with supporting the family at home.

"What do you mean? Of course, I will relax. Sometimes, I will visit the kids and sometimes they will visit us. We are old now. We have had our lives already and this is the time to watch.

Thank God, the routine is over. I mean the routine of getting up in the morning and rushing to work and sleeping and then getting up to go to that boring job every day. I did everything for the children and I am happy that they are doing fine with their lives. What contentment it is!

You are also an old woman now. Do not exert too much. Would you like a full time maid? I can afford one you know, thanks to the reasonable pension I will continue to receive from my company. And then, for money matters, we can always ask our children, I hope they will not say no. What do you think?"

"Yes, even I think they will not say no. But I do not think that we should ask them for money. It is such an expensive life these days and they have their own expenses to take care of. I do not need a maid anyways. I need some work to keep going. What will I do otherwise! The household work had never been too stressing for me."

"Okay, your wish."

Rakesh started spending his days reading, watching TV, chatting, eating and sleeping. He was happy going to the neighbourhood park in the morning and chat with people like him. Once back from the park, he would stay at home for the rest of the day.

A month went by. And a few more passed. He did not ask himself how he felt as a retired man. He did not know why. May be he felt that the question was scary and he would not really enjoy listening to the answer.

One day, he thought: I am still 60. I retired 6 months back and it feels that I have been at home for years. I have no idea how long am I going to live. I do not know. This is something that I do not choose. So, let's say that I have 20 more years to go, even if I have 10 more years to go, how do I intend to spend my time? Can I survive like this or is it worth it at all?

The questions disturbed him.

That day, one of his old friends visited him. They had been friends since college. His name was Chintan Patel.

Chintan was a businessman. He was 62, that is, two years elder to Rakesh. He looked in prime state of mental and physical health.

"So, how are things Rakesh. I heard you retired from your job?"

"Yes, Chintan, you heard it right. I am doing fine, relaxing at home after working for the entire life. Now, I just want to take it easy."

"Oh, so you mean that your life is virtually over now."

"No, I do not mean that. What do you mean by that?"

"That is what I understand by what you say. You want to relax. How much relaxation do you need, for example? How have you been spending your time and how do you intend to spend it from here?"

"Well, I have been reading, spending time with my neighbours, visiting the park, watching TV, among other things."

"I see. And you intend to do this till the last day of your life, do you?"

"I do not know. I have not thought about it."

"Look, Rakesh, I am not saying that it is incorrect to relax. Of course, you have spent a long working life and have money at your disposal. Your kids are doing fine. They do not need your money either. But, why would you want to get busy dying?"

"What the hell do you mean?!"

"You see Rakesh; either we are busy living or busy dying. When people ask me if I have any plans to retire, the question does not make sense to me. I have a business which I started many years back. The business has expanded and I have delegated the majority of responsibility to my two sons. They take care of the operations and the finances. But I still provide directional guidance to the business. I am also involved in social projects which give me immense satisfaction. I have started an NGO which helps underprivileged children.

I do not intend to retire from work. I mean, work is my life. If I do not work, what am I supposed to do, watch TV and waste precious time of my life?"

"I don't know Chintan. Everyone is not like you. There are so many people who make different decisions and accordingly spend their time."

"Well, okay, it's your choice, after all. You have my business card. If you need to talk anytime about how you may usefully want to use your time, call me."

"Okay, I will. I will think about it, thanks."

"Great. I will get going now. I have things to attend to. It was nice meeting you Rakesh after a long time. Take care of yourselves."

Rakesh shrugged off the discussion after Chintan left. Why should everyone think like he does anyway? He decided to watch a movie and forget about it.

"I do not want to work anymore. Chintan is a madman," he told himself.

***

One morning when he went for his early morning walk in the park, he saw that his acquaintances in the park were whispering about something very slowly. The topic seemed to be tragic. He joined in the discussion, curious to know what had transpired that had everyone huddled up. They were not taking a walk as usual or discussing politics. Something grave had happened.

"Who was he? He lived in the lane next to Mr. Sharma's?"

"Oh, yes. He lived there. He used to stand at the intersection to drop his grandson at the bus stop. He used to stand there every day," went the discussion, thus.

"His name was Suraj Raj. He took early retirement 3 years back and since then he spent his time at home. Yesterday in the evening, he got angry with a vegetable vendor and it lead to a bitter argument. He was shouting at him when he suddenly collapsed. Apparently, he had a heart attack. He never woke up."

"Yes, it is possible. Nobody understands why these things happen. He looked absolutely fine and if one looked at him, one could never say that he would die of a heart attack. It is so surprising."

Suraj had died of a heart attack. Rakesh knew Suraj briefly. They had had a few small chats and he had seen him many times going accompanying his grandson to the bus stop. He could not forget Suraj's face. He had had a very pleasant smile with which he would greet Rakesh.

That morning, Rakesh went home in a state of numbness. Something inside him had moved.

When he reached home, he looked in a state of shock. His wife looked concerned and asked him what had happened?

"Nothing has happened. The world is fine. Everything is ok. Nothing has changed. Suraj has died."

"What nonsense are you talking? Who was Suraj and how does it bother you that he died? I do not remember any friend of yours with that name."

"Yes, he was not my friend. How does it matter after all?"

His wife thought that he was turning senile and moved on with her work. Rakesh kept on thinking about Suraj for the rest of the day. He did not know why it should bother him after all.

At the end of the day, he realised what he needed to do. Next morning, after his walk and breakfast, he picked up the phone and called Chintan.

"Hello Rakesh. How are you?"

"Hello Chintan. I do not want to be busy dying, not any more. Can I come and see you today?"

"Sure you can. Come to see me any time in my office."

Chintan badly needed someone to support him with his philanthropic activities-someone he could trust and Rakesh was like a godsend for him. They started working on the NGO to reach underprivileged children and provide them a better childhood.

Rakesh felt extremely excited about what he was doing now. He felt that all his life his desk job did not provide him the opportunity to work with people from different walks of society and build relationships that are based on trust and contribution. He could not describe the feeling of having been of use to the children.

All of them called him Rakesh uncle and he loved them. His time now went in raising funds for the efforts, thinking about new activities that they could do to enrich young lives and to talk about something to the media that he was so proud of.

The work that he was doing made him feel young and alive. He smiled much more than he used to. He actually laughed so much that he surprised himself.

He gave up all thoughts about retiring ever again. He did not want to stop. Although there were limits to what he could do physically because of his age, but he was determined never to let his age stop him mentally.

He did not sit in the park anymore to discuss politics. He did not watch TV. He did not read women's magazines. He did not have the time anymore.

He had better things to do.

He wanted to live his life completely before he would pass away. This was an exciting time for him. All his life, he had worked because he had wanted the money. Now, he did not need the money. He had enough to spend the rest of his life in his bed. Now, he could work for reasons other than money. He could spend his time generating smiles on the faces of young kids. He felt that it took him very long to connect with himself at a deeper level. Thankfully, he could connect with his soul now.

That is, before he died."

"Age is just a useless number. It does not mean anything. The meaning you decide to give to it is the meaning of your age. You are as old or young as you think you are."

-Amar

10. Death

Death is the single best invention of life

- Steve Jobs (Stanford Commencement speech 2005)

I think about death a lot. Do you think it's morbid to you? I am a healthy 39 years man! Why should I be thinking about death?

I do not see it that way. I don't think it's morbid. I think the only absolute truth no man can deny is that "one day, he is going to die."

Science has not been able to find any solution to the human problem of death and no man or woman who took birth has lived forever. Life gives way to life. Someone dies and a child is born somewhere else.

I do not think the pursuit of eternity is worth it either.

If we know that we are not going to die, we will not value life.

The fact that life can be and will be snatched away from us any moment by an invisible power makes us realise the value of life. It tells us that we have been allotted a limited life span and we must make the most of it. And, it is absolutely unfair. We have not been given any deadlines. We, human beings, the creatures of logic and rationale, have not been given a fair deal. We, the most powerful creatures on the planet, cannot do anything about it!

You see, how helpless we are when it comes to death!

You are going to die. Does this statement scare you?

Let me say this again.

You are going to die any moment.

There is no guarantee that you will see tomorrow. When that moment comes, it would not matter if you are happy or sad. It would not matter who you are. It would not matter what you have accomplished in life or what you think you want to accomplish. Your entire existence will come to an end suddenly and you will not be there to notice it.

You will not be a part of this world any longer. Your body will be burnt or buried. The spirit will be eliminated. I have no idea where it will go after that.

It is only through the unchallenged acceptance of this truth that we may die any minute, we realise the true essence of life

-Amar

Death can come in any shape. It can come in the form of a tsunami, hurricane, earthquake, accident, heart attack, cancer, electrocution, diabetes, drug overdose, over exertion and myriad other forms. Do you understand how creative it is and how many shapes it can take?

What really matters is that you won't know when it hits you. It will when it is supposed to. Unfortunately, some fortune tellers may fool you into believing that they can tell you when you are going to die, trust them at your own peril.

I have seen many people die over the years. As is usual of me, I asked a question- 'Why did they have to die when they died?'

You may ask me, "Why would I want to ask this question?"

Let me give you the answer. I ask this question to figure out what is it that gives me the right to be alive right now when I have seen people younger to me die! I do not understand. I do not think they were bad people. Some of them had amazing lives right in front of them. There was no comprehensible reason to die. But they died.

They are not a part of this world anymore. It baffles my mind. I will take an example.

Ishmeet Singh died when he was just 20. People who watch reality shows in India would know his name. He was the winner of a reality TV show in India-The Voice of India. It was July 29, 2008 and I was in the business school. I have a post on my blog dated that day with the question-"why did he have to die?"

I chose him as an example since he was young and successful. Had he been alive today, he would have been enjoying the beauty that life has to offer- success, travel, friends and love. He was a star in a country of over a billion people at such a young age. It was a spectacular life in the making. He drowned in a pool in Maldives.

Two of my seniors at S P Jain Center of Management- Malayesh and Gaurav lost their lives on 26/11. They were at the Leopold Cafe. Two extremely bright lives were lost for no conceivable reason. I remember their smiling faces vividly.

Many such incidents have left indelible marks on my conscious. They have influenced the way I think about death. I do not live in an insulated world. Everything that happens around me, affects me.

You would also know someone in your sphere of existence that died young and unannounced. I know many. Some of them were brothers or sisters of my friends, someone studied with me in the same school. It's bizarre but it is for real.

Death is inevitable and imminent. No matter how big you think you are, it will hit you with a fatal blow.

What will happen after that?

People who love you will cry for a few days and then they will move ahead with their lives. *What will remain is the impact you left on your fellow beings while you stayed in this world.*

Leave a positive impact. Touch a few lives. Say some beautiful words. Hug everyone you love and care for. Choose to smile and make the world a better place. Do everything you can with the gifts bestowed upon you to improve your own life and add positivity and kindness to the lives to people around you.

The only people who do not have problems, anxieties and apprehensions are dead. Would you want to be there?

There are so many people who die before they can learn what it feels to get older, would you want to be one of them?

Let me tell you a story

Remember Roshan, he died in the first chapter of this book.

He reached the heavens.

When he confronted his creator, Roshan asked him, "Why did I die so soon? I was too young to die. My parents must be grieving."

"My son, I love you and that is why I called you back. You were not happy on earth. People were not treating you well and I did not want to see you unhappy. I want to see you happy. That is why you are back, safe with me.

Go and enjoy yourself," the creator said this much and disappeared.

Roshan looked around. There was a door right in front of him. He opened it and walked out.

This is it, he thought.

This was heaven.

It was a fascinating place with mind stupefying beauty. There was a blue water beach right in front of Roshan gleaming against the sunset. The retreating rays of the sun were falling on the blue water.

A young boy of his age passed by and said, "Hi, how are you?"

"Hi, I am good, thanks."

The boy moved on, smiling at Roshan.

Roshan moved towards the beach. He took his slippers off and walked into water. There were many people around. They were all smiling and cheering. It was an amazing place. He looked at the water. There were fish touching his legs.

"They will not bite you, don't worry," one old man said, as he moved his hand on Roshan's head.

"Thank you, uncle, for comforting me. I am new here. I died this morning."

"Oh I see. I have been here for many years. Consider me like your grandfather. I can take care of you if you want. I died in an accident. I was a businessman and had amassed a lot of money on earth. I used to give it away to poor people. There are many foundations running in my name. I was living in America. It is a big country. They call it the land of dreams."

"How nice Uncle. I have never met anyone from America. How are you and I in the same place? My father used to tell me that you need visa to meet people from America."

Oh, that is true on earth. *On heaven, there are no boundaries and no geographies divided among countries. The area of heaven is 100 times that of earth and you are free to move anywhere you like.*

You will meet people of multiple colours, races and backgrounds. They all live happily together. Diversity is celebrated. No one thinks that a white man is superior to a black man. I was never able to understand this attitude on earth as well. So, you do not need a visa to meet anyone.

And everyone who comes to heaven was a nice man or woman on earth. The creator loves these people also and hence he calls them to heaven."

"Yes, he told me the same thing also. Where would I eat and live?"

"Oh, don't worry. In heaven, the food and accommodation is provided for by the government of heaven and hell (GOHAH). So, basically, people do not have to work for money."

"Uncle, what do you know about hell?"

"Oh, why do you want to know?"

"Just like that, out of curiosity."

"You children, ask a lot of questions! Okay, I will tell you. Hell is a wretched place. People who intentionally cause pain to others are damned to hell! They get what they deserve there. They are made to work in menial jobs by demons and beaten if they do not do their job. They are not given food for many days and it completely depends on the intentions of demons how they decide to treat those people.

The government of heaven and hell decides who will go to heaven and hell when they die and those people who go to hell stay there forever since they are at the mercy of demons. The government has decided that people who will give pain to others intentionally will have to bear pain themselves. I do not want to talk about it anymore. It is a bad world out there."

"No problem, grandpa. Thank you for telling me what you did. I am thankful that I have come to the heaven. I do not know why the GOHAH decided that I should go to heaven and not hell.

I am not sure if I was an ideal child. I caused a lot of pain to my parents. I never intended to cause any pain to them. They loved me so much. I loved them also. But I could not stand up to their expectations. I caused them pain. I should have gone to hell!"

The old man had tears in his eyes on hearing this.

He said, "No, my son. You did not cause any pain to them intentionally. You did your best by trying to score well but they unintentionally created pressure on you which made your life as bit difficult.

I know it myself. I was not a great father. I think I should have done much better. My son wanted to be a painter. I did not allow him to work to be one till he was 25. He suffered a nervous breakdown but thankfully he survived and that is when I realised where I was going wrong. When he recovered, I let him do what he wanted. He is a very successful painter now. He lives in London."

"Thank you Grandpa, you make me feel so comfortable."

"You are welcome, my son."

"What will I do here?"

"Why, anything you like doing. Just do what you like, what makes you happy, what you enjoy doing."

"Is it?! Can I just do what I like?"

"Yes, just do what you like. That's what everyone does here. Make friends with people. They will help you. Do not doubt their intentions. You can trust them that they will not betray you and that they are genuine."

"Wow, this is a wonderful world."

"Yes, my son, it is wonderful world. Actually, life at earth could be wonderful also and many of these rules that GOHAH has applied here can be applied there as well. But humans have a tendency to make their lives complicated. They behave as if it is a sin to be happy and a virtue to be miserable.

The entire society is designed that way and so are the laws. People who oppose or dissent are silenced or not listened to.

I hope one day better sense will prevail at earth also. It is a gift to be given the life of a human being. Human beings are the most powerful creatures on earth for they can use the power of will or volition to create their life the way they want.

Happiness is not in the acquisition of money. Yes, money is important to lead a fulfilling life but it is just one of the tools. Blatant pursuit of money will only lead to misery.

There is so much work to be done on earth. It can only be done by human beings. Only human beings can help their fellow beings.

It is their responsibility to make their world a better place to live in. Amen"

End of story

The Whisper of Death

One day I was sitting alone

And I heard a sound whispering in my ears

I asked, 'who are you?'

The voice said, 'I am your end, I am death

I am here to give you a message

Listen carefully-

I walk with you, like your shadow

And will touch you one day…

You don't know where and when

So, here is my advice to you

Before I do

Live your life with as much intensity as you can

With as much intensity as you can

The End

9 798653 531941